I0710192

Veiled Phoenix

By

Huckleberry Rahr

Copyright © 2024 Huckleberry Rahr
All rights reserved.

The characters and events portrayed in this book are fictitious. Any similarity to real persons, living or dead, is coincidental and not intended by the author.

No part of this book may be reproduced, or stored in a retrieval system, or transmitted in any form or by any means, electronic, mechanical, photocopying, recording, or otherwise, without express written permission of the publisher.

No part of this book was created, written, or otherwise conceptualized by AI.

ISBN eBook: 978-1-959981-57-2
ISBN paperback: 978-1-959981-58-9

Developmental Editor: Angela Grimes
Cover Art: Getcovers.com
Formatting: Huckleberry Rahr

Books In the Ember Savita Series

1: Veiled Phoenix

2: Moonstone Phoenix

3: Battle Phoenix

Books by Huckleberry Rahr

- Jade Stone Chronicles
  - Wolf Healer
  - Epsilon
  - Alphas
  - Traitor
  - Pack
  - Battlefield
  - Pack Present
- Pebble Stone Chronicles
  - Xenagogue
  - Yugen
  - Zephyr
- Ember Savita Chronicles
  - Veiled Phoenix
  - Moonstone Phoenix
  - Battle Phoenix
- The Search – Short Story, eBook only

Acknowledgements

When I started writing, I never imagined where I'd end up. The people in the community are more than amazing. At the beginning, I thought Wolf Healer and Epsilon would be it. The fact that you are about to start my second series tells you how wrong I was.

I always have to thank some of my biggest supporters, those people who are with me every day, encouraging me, cheering me on, and helping me when I'm not sure why my characters have gone as far afield as they've gone. I'll start with the OG of my writing group: Angela Grimes, Weslee Imrisek, and Lawrence Henry.

When the four of us started our group, along with Haydee ... who's still there, but very busy, I hadn't even published my first book ... none of us had. Now we all have books running amok in the world.

There have been others who have joined our small group, some have moved on, but Nicole and Juanita Maness are here to stay. They read my rough drafts and are free with positive words of encouragement.

Well, in the end, I hope you enjoy this new series. It was a challenge with a nonbinary main character, but I really love this world. I hope you do as well!

To my readers

Ember Savita, the main character of this series, is nonbinary. They use they/them pronouns. There were a couple of nonbinary characters in the Jade Stone Chronicles, so I knew this path wouldn't be simple. As I wrote this book, I was excited to create this main character.

Writing a character with they/them pronouns is a challenge. I may have made some mistakes. If I did, I apologize. This book has been critiqued and edited by many people, but I'm sure some mistakes still found their way through.

Thank you for joining me on this journey. I appreciate all of you.

Chapter 1 - My Parents Made Me Do It

Ember

Ember held their shaking hand over a tray of dirt, muscles tense, eyes narrowed, as they attempted for ... something ... anything. They bit their lip and focused on trying to get a shape to form out of the pile of earth sitting on their desk. *Why did I get put in this dumb proficiency anyway? I'm already the laughingstock of the school. This doesn't make things any better.* Gut clenched, jaw aching, all they wanted was some indication that they could do an inkling of earth magic.

They reminded themself that they didn't care what others thought of them. School was about learning, not bullies. Who cared if the mean, popular students didn't like them? Some days, that belief was easier than others.

Back to the soil.

Sweat began to form on their forehead and along their spine as they tensed their abs. *I wonder if this counts as a workout?*

Mom's voice floated up the stairs. "Ember, can you come to the kitchen?"

Every muscle relaxed, their arm collapsed into their lap, and they slumped in their seat. "Homework!" Ember yelled back, hearing the stress in their own voice.

"I'll send something up." Moments later, a cup of tea appeared next to them on the desk, along with painkillers. They sighed. Mom's voice came again, this time filled with concern. "We need to speak with you soon, love, and dinner will be done in ten minutes."

Ember sipped their tea, took the meds, and tried to relax. They glared at their nemesis ... the pile of earth. It didn't quake in fear, despite using their fiercest face.

"Fine. Ten minutes." Ember calmed the snap in their voice, forcing themself to sound pleasant. It wasn't Mom's fault they failed at such a simple task. *Why is this easy for most earth magic witches?*

After a deep breath, they held their hand over the dirt again. With a frustrated snarl, they flicked their hand and watched as fire cover their fingers. Holding the blaze in place, Ember slid their fingers out from the flames, then, making a fist, transformed the fire into a sphere. They sipped their tea as they shrank the fireball down into the shape of a marble. When they rotated their arm, the ball spun and morphed into the shape of a heart before it dissipated.

Ember took a sip of tea and let it warm them before setting down the mug and glaring at the tray. Now that the use of fire magic had released a bit of their tension, they were ready to focus on harder stuff. Earth magic basics.

They hovered both hands above the tray and concentrated as much as they could. A shiver of power ran down their spine, and a small lump the size of their thumb appeared in the dirt. Leaping up, Ember's jaw dropped.

They ran to their phone and checked the footage. They'd set it up on a tripod to record what they were doing, hoping to have some proof they could do earth magic. They weren't sure who they were trying to prove it to—themself, their friends, maybe their teacher—but they needed something to convince themself to try in this magical proficiency. The dirt lump growing from the flat tray was there ... but so was the fire show.

Why do things have to be so difficult?

"Damn it all to Hades and back!"

Ember grabbed their tea and headed down to join their parents for dinner. Both Mom and Dad waited, Mom by the stove filling bowls and Dad sitting at the round kitchen table. Ember flopped into a seat and slid their phone across the table. "Dad, I finally got the earth to move, but"—they blushed—"it also picked up some fire magic. Can you do some editing?"

Dad beamed, joy emanating from his face. "You performed earth magic? For real? Congratulations! And of course. Let me see what I can do."

After he spoke, Mom said, "I knew you could do it, hon. You're my kid. The power had to be in there somewhere! We should celebrate. After dinner we'll walk down to the ice cream shop."

"It only took me sixteen years! I don't know if what I created can be defined as anything more than a fluke, but, well, it wasn't nothing, and you know I won't turn down ice cream."

Dad grabbed the phone while Mom served jambalaya. "Well, I'm proud of you." The spicy aroma brought a grumble from Ember's belly.

They leapt up. "Drinks?"

Mom smiled. "I have red wine for me and Dad. Go ahead and get yourself something. There's an important school topic we need to discuss with you."

The pep in Ember's step slowed as they went to the fridge and selected a soda. "Should I be worried?" Ember went to the cupboard for a glass, filled it with their drink, and sat back down at the table.

"No, don't be worried, but food first, and then we'll talk." The talking stopped while everyone enjoyed the food.

Though dinner was excellent, Ember's mind kept circling about what their parents wanted to discuss. It cast a shadow over the whole meal.

When bowls were mostly empty, Mom placed her utensil down. "Okay, Ember, it's time to talk."

A chill snaked down Ember's spine, though they were glad to finally get to the topic at hand. "What's up, Mom?"

"The school sent me and Dad emails. Apparently, there's a field trip coming up soon, and they were worried that we were refusing to allow you to go. Apparently, it's a pretty big deal for your grade." She took a sip of her wine. "You never told us anything about it, love. You never gave us the permission slip to sign. Talk to me, Ember."

Ember closed their eyes for a moment and sighed. *So close to avoiding all of this. How did I forget about emails?*

Ember bit their cheek and put down their fork. "I don't want to go."

Dad slid the phone back across the table. "Why not? We didn't raise you to hide from a challenge."

They slumped. "Everyone else has known each other their whole lives, and I'm still the 'new kid.' Everyone else has friends." Ember shrugged. "And there are stories of pranks. It just doesn't seem like my thing."

Mom's eyes softened. "You have friends. You and Daisy have been best friends since you moved here. You two are practically inseparable! And Felix? I would think having a boyfriend would count as having a friend, and he's a great kid. Even Dad thinks so."

Crossing their arms, Ember let their head drop back. "I know. I just worry about the stories I've heard. Kids aren't monitored, so magic and mayhem run rampant. I don't have much that I can do or use for protection. And camping .... We'll be out in the woods for two nights. I just ... I don't want to 'people' that much. School is about my limit."

Dad leaned forward. "You *can* protect yourself. And Felix's magic is strong. Daisy isn't as powerful, but she's good. The three of you will be fine together. Please be honest, Ember. What is it you're worried about?"

"I just ... I'm not sure about showing the other kids that I can do more magic. I'm in the classes for earth magic, and I can't really do anything there. I'm known for my inabilities there. I have my air magic ... but I hide most of that, and then there's my fire—"

"Your fire magic," Dad interrupted, "is stronger than any teacher's in that building. You can't let anyone know how good you are. I don't think you can dumb down your fire to a point that you present as merely great. You do fine with air magic, but you don't have any reference point for fire."

"Yeah, I know."

Mom sighed. "Your air magic is top-notch. You just decided to hide that to brush up on the basics that I never taught you. But it's been three years, Ember. Do you really think that's still the right decision?"

"I don't know, and even if I decided to do better, wouldn't that be splashy? People would ask questions. It would be weird. I just want to blend in." They waved their hands in circles.

Mom's expression softened. "I know. School is hard, and kids can be mean. Fading into the background can be nice, but it isn't always possible. Eventually, you'll need to actually show them what you can do with your air proficiency. Who knows, maybe you'll learn something new. They taught you the basics in the first year. Now, it's your time to shine. Maybe they can really challenge you."

Ember slumped. "Yeah, maybe. I'll think about it. Though, I doubt they can challenge me more than you do."

Dad turned to Mom. "Do you know where I left my water?"

Ember saw it on the counter behind the coffee maker. "I got it." They put up their hand, thumb up, pinky down, and waved the bottom half, like telling someone to move ahead. With a small push of will, the water shifted from the counter to the table in front of Dad.

"Honey, you're getting better control over your spatial magic. Have you been practicing?"

"A little. I use it around here whenever I find an excuse. Mom set up a practice schedule for all my free time." They said the last with a bit of a groan. What teen liked more study during free time?

Sipping her wine, Mom leaned back. "Stop trying to change the subject. We need to focus on the field trip. I think you should go. Now, I'm printing off the permission slip, and I'll sign it. Learning about night ingredients for potions and harvesting them is a skill you should have."

Ember grumbled, "I have a copy of the paper in my backpack. You don't have to print it off."

After dinner, Ember found the permission slip. They'd delayed getting it signed almost to the deadline, but alas, technology was their enemy. They were going to be harvesting midnight spell components whether they wanted to or not.

Chapter 2 - Are You Human or Witch?

Ember

Ember trudged to first period on Monday.

Daisy bopped along next to them, happy as could be. Her long brown hair bounced, and her blue eyes danced. She loved school and mastering her magic. "And then Mom told me about this article she read about a new uprising and how the humans are gathering to subjugate the magic users. She said it was all balderdash, but I don't know. She thinks I should add it to the report as a warning about history repeating itself, but I was like, Mom, the report is like, history, not current events, and she was like–"

"Stop, wait, what?" Ember's head hurt too much for this. They loved their friend, but her morning energy was sometimes too much. "Something is happening now that relates to our assignment?"

"Yes, silly, haven't you been listening? The humans are starting to get scared about how powerful we are. They're banding together to fight us. It's something altogether new. You need to get your head out of the clouds and pay attention. I know you like to avoid social media, but really, Ember, pay attention."

Ember bit back a laugh as they navigated around a group of students milling about in the hall. They couldn't believe that this came from Daisy. As smart as Daisy was and as good as her grades were, she got *too* much information from suspicious sources. When Ember got home, they'd do some of their own research. *If it just came from Daisy, I'd blow it off, but if she's also getting it from her mom, there may be something there.*

Ember weaved around a group of students sitting against their lockers, feet sticking out into the hall. It was mad, the number of people dashing to class versus others lollygagging about as if they had all the time in the world.

Felix caught up to them, wrapping his arm around Ember's shoulders. Ember shot him a glance. His light-brown hair was perfectly styled. They loved that it matched his eye color. "It's in more places than social media, Daisy." He obviously had heard them talking. "This new uprising is crazy. I don't know how anyone can believe any of it, since it *started* on the extremist sites." He sighed. "In the original war where humans learned about magic and shapeshifters, we lost a lot of good people. But in the end, we've had peace. I don't think these new rumors are starting with the humans as the sites all say. It's all garbage."

Well, if Felix knows about it, there must be more to the story.

Daisy raised a brow at him. "It did start with the humans. Do your research, Felix! You're usually smarter than this! And as for the last war, you *know* that there are still shapeshifters in the world, just not as many as there were before the last wave of that battle. You've done enough research over the years."

Ember hated these discussions, the two of them fighting over things that didn't need to be fought about. Ember put their hands out as if to separate their friends. "Yes, there are shapeshifters, but not as many as there used to be, either in number or variety." Their voice dropped as other students stared at the trio. "Some species completely died out. Can we please just get to class without a full-on fight?" Ember looked at their two closest friends beseechingly. "Please."

"Most of them died off," Felix mumbled, probably too soft for Daisy to hear.

Swinging around, Daisy stuck a finger into Felix's chest. "You're just upset because the phoenixes all became extinct. You've been obsessed ever since that report you did in year five." Daisy turned to Ember. "It was cute back then. Now, not so much."

Ember didn't know either of them back in year five. They'd moved to the area for secondary school in year nine. "*Are* you obsessed with phoenixes? It's a weird obsession, you know." They couldn't help but tease their boyfriend. Then they turned to Daisy. "I mean, if he is obsessed, he's doing a poor job of it if I haven't heard hide nor hair in all these years, or would it be feather nor tail?"

"No." He shook his head. "I just think it's sad that we lost so many different kinds of magic and magical beasts. Can you imagine? Before the war two hundred years ago, we thought that most of the shapeshifters, especially the phoenixes, were immortal. The only reason the phoenixes died was because they sacrificed themselves in pairs so that their death fire wouldn't become Everfire."

Ember licked their lips. Most people didn't know that much about phoenixes. "Everfire?"

Daisy groaned. "Do *not* get him started! I didn't have enough coffee this morning to deal with Felix all giddy about phoenixes and their sacrifices."

"Everfire is the death fire of the phoenix. When a phoenix normally dies, they burn up and are reborn. When they die a true death, the kind they can't come back from, their fire becomes Everfire, something that burns super-hot and destroys everything it touches. And, fun fact, it never burns out. If you kill a single phoenix, and their death fire, the Everfire, touches you, instant death to that person. So, anyone who hunted phoenixes in the past had to both know about the Everfire and how to contain it."

Ember nodded slowly. "That's incredible, and interesting. How did you learn all this?"

"There's more. Apparently if they die in pairs, their fire doesn't become Everfire. Anyway, in the last war, the phoenixes flew in as their birds, and, okay, I don't know the exact details, but they had a way to die together so their fire wasn't eternal. It's fantastic." Somehow Felix missed their question, lost in his lesson.

A sadness made Ember miss a step. They weren't sure how the sacrifice and death of a species was fantastic. All those birds, all those *people*, died, to ensure peace. Ember knew why it had happened, but the idea that the majestic beings were gone hurt deep inside. Steeling themselves, Ember shook their head. As they continued to class, they fought to hide their emotions about the loss of life. They couldn't explain to their friends why this topic made them emotional.

Daisy grabbed Ember's hand and dragged them towards class. "See, he's obsessed. What did I tell you? Next time, listen to me, and don't get him started!"

Ember smiled at Felix. "I think I know what you did your report for Magical History on. My angle was on the different shifter species that helped to ensure the final success of the war, but I only touched on the phoenixes. There were others to discuss as well."

A bounce entered Felix's step. "You wrote about their sacrifice? If it weren't for the shifters, the humans wouldn't be free today. It was all the shifters, but especially the phoenixes. They led the armies."

"There aren't any real details to support that." Daisy sighed. "You're just assuming this is true because you want it to be true."

Felix's head drooped to the side, and he made a disappointed sound. "You know how to ruin a guy's morning, Daisy."

The three of them made it to class. It was being held outside in the West Field so they could all access the earth.

Whereas this helped most of the class, for Ember, it just highlighted their inability to use earth magic.

Well, here goes nothing ... probably literally. Another day, another class where I can make a fool of myself being the only one in class unable to perform.

As they approached, Josie sneered at them. Her spiky brown hair didn't move in the wind. "Well, if it isn't our resident human pretending to be a magic user. Ember Savita, are you going to wow us with your ability to hold out your hand and what, tremble?" She walked over and flicked Ember's long, wavy auburn hair. "Maybe you're in the wrong class with this red hair? You've never seemed to be able to do much here." She turned to Cress, another of the popular bullies. "Are there any witches with red hair? Have we figured that out in all our years here?"

He smirked. "I've only seen that color in humans. Our kind doesn't crossbreed with ... them, so no, they must be a wannabe taking up space in our school."

A few other students laughed. It sounded forced.

Josie leaned in, her green eyes inches away from Ember. "I don't know why you attend this school. Is there any magic in you at all?"

Daisy shot forward. "Of course they can do magic. They test all the students. What, do you think you're better than the teachers and officials?"

"Oh, Daisy, aren't you just the sweetest guard dog ever? Why don't you go off and sniff a tree." Josie gave a feminine snort before turning her back on Daisy.

With a squealing huff, Daisy shot daggers at Josie. "You do not get to tell me what to do."

"Okay, everyone, in a circle," the teacher interrupted, walking up from the school.

Ember's heart dropped. In this configuration, everyone would see them fail at whatever task was put in front of them. They liked rows much better.

"Let's start with each of you creating a seat out of the dirt. Pull it up from the soil so you can sit." He went on to describe the requirement, taking up several minutes of class.

Once it was time to work, Ember watched as students did different motions to call on their magic. Everyone had a different tell. Josie waved her hand and pulled up a throne. Felix barely put out his fingers and pulled up a bench. Daisy held out her hands and pulled up what looked like a recliner chair. All around them, the earth gave up seats.

Putting out their hand, Ember poured energy towards the ground, trying for something, anything. With the project being enough earth that a person could sit on it, everyone took time to create their masterpiece. Ember wondered if everyone would finish before class ended.

Just the day before, they'd pulled up a bit of soil in their room. Their head began to pound with the beating of their heart, and they shut their eyes. They felt sweat drip down their back as their arms shook. *Please, let this work, let me finally get something.*

They scrunched up their face, made a fist, and pulled. Jaw clenched, Ember looked to the ground. For once, they'd done something. A small lump of dirt no bigger than a jewelry box sat on the ground, mocking them.

For a moment, Ember's joy soared. They'd done it! There, sitting on the ground, was the proof that they could do ... something. It was tiny, but evidence. Relief washed through them as a small smile played across their face. *This is probably what year two students do, but it proves I can do something.*

As they gazed down at the small lump of dirt, barely an inch in height, pride swelled in their chest. *I finally did a thing in class. Dad would be so happy for me. Mom may buy me a cupcake!*

They wanted to pound their fist into the air, but searching the other student's achievements, they knew what they had was a complete failure.

A loud guffaw erupted from behind, and Ember barely turned in time to see Josie throw her head back laughing. "What is that? Are you creating a hovel stool for your dolls? I bet you still play with dolls. Is that what you and Daisy do on the weekends? God, you're pathetic."

The girl stomped over then leaned down. "Did you just kick a lump of dirt over? This is seriously a sad showing."

Standing up, Josie's upper lip rose in a sneer towards Ember. "You don't deserve to be here."

Ember heard a thump, and looking down, they saw Josie's foot where their meager achievement had been.

Chapter 3 - A Muddy Throne

Daisy

Daisy watched as Ember shut their eyes and spun on their heels to leave. *Did their eyes ... flash red for a moment before they shut them? No, I'm imagining things.* "What the hell, Josie? Why couldn't you let Ember have their success? Are you so threatened by them?" *She is always such a bully! Why can't she just leave Ember alone?*

She'd had to deal with Josie her whole life. They'd been neighbors, and when they were kids, they'd been friends. Then, in second grade, Josie became popular. After that, she'd used everything she knew about Daisy to gain more popularity. A real viper.

Daisy watched as her friend headed back to the school, back stiff and head held high. Class wasn't over, but it was close enough. The teacher, once again, had missed Josie's antics. Somehow that girl had always gotten away with her nastiness. That was her other skill, never getting caught. *One day, a teacher will see her.*

"Oh, it's the guard dog again." Josie's voice dripped from her like poison bubbling out of a cauldron.

As much as Josie's words stung, she knew the nasty girl was more of a lapdog to the popular crowd than anyone in the school. She rolled her eyes at the bully. "Whatever," she mumbled, refusing to let the other girl get to her.

Josie smirked as she continued. "What did you do before you had your little redheaded friend to protect? Barking and snarling? Oh, that's right, you're such a loyal friend because before Ember, you didn't have any friends."

"Is there a reason you're so obsessed with me, Josie? Why have you been spending all your time watching my every move?" One of Daisy's eyebrows shot up in challenge.

Felix came up to them, his voice low. "Enough, Josie. Haven't you caused enough trouble? Why don't you go back to your monstrosity of a throne?" He flicked his hand as if dismissing her, but the throne crumbled.

"Oh my god! What did you do!" She ran. When she got to the throne, it snapped back into place.

"What *did* you do?" Daisy narrowed her eyes. She knew he didn't have an affinity of water. That was her thing. *What had he done?* "Oh, wait, you just made us see something that wasn't there, didn't you? Mind magic." She smiled, approving of his antics.

He chuckled. "She needs to be given a bit of her own medicine once in a while."

"Do you think Ember's okay?" Worry thrummed through her. She knew from air magic class that Ember had abilities. They may not be the best in the school, but they *were* a witch. *Why don't they just show the bullies and shut them up?* She'd asked Ember to prove themself a few times in their first and second years, but they'd refused, saying they didn't care what others thought. Daisie finally gave up trying to push her friend.

"I think they'll be fine. We'll talk to them next period." He headed back to his bench.

The teacher made it to Daisy's recliner and she smiled, excitement coursing through her. She loved showing off her work, especially to teachers. School had always been one of her favorite places to be, despite the other students. Josie hadn't been wrong that Ember had been her first real friend in years. Ember was real and honest, a true friend. They'd never lie to her.

He circled her recliner. "Nice work, as always. Can the footrest pop out?"

Scrunching up her face, she created a pull bar and offered him the first try. As he yanked it down, she focused on having a bit of dirt rise from the bottom and the back lower. It made her a bit dizzy, but the effect was perfect. She'd expended a lot of magic, but it was worth it. The result was amazing.

"That is some of your best work, Ms. Autumn." He searched the area around her. "Where is Ember?"

Dread filled Daisy. She wanted to get Josie in trouble, but in eleven years of school, she knew that it would never work out. Clenching her jaw, she took a deep breath and then put on her best smile. "They felt queasy. They worried they may throw up, so they headed for the restroom. Believe it or not, they created a small mound, but it got trampled in some excitement. I'm sorry you missed it."

He nodded. "Thanks for the information. Why don't you pack up and check on them. If need be, they should see the nurse. Let them know I hope they feel better, and I'll see them on Wednesday for class." He moved on to check over Felix's work.

With a sigh, Daisy wanted to flop into her chair but didn't want to get quite that muddy. She wondered if it would be hard to find Ember, but her friend was just inside the school. "You okay?"

"I just ... why ... how does Josie get away with being so mean all the time?"

"I don't know. She always has." Daisy gave Ember a hug.

"Thanks. I just need to not cry before second period. Let's start walking. I want to put off seeing her for as long as possible."

"Sure, let's go." Daisy hoped Ember would be okay before next period, because there were too many opinionated and popular people in their next class. Ember's apparent lack of magic had been an issue for three years, and with this new division with humans coming up, Daisy worried about her friend. *I know Ember has magic. They wouldn't be here if they didn't ... I saw the earth lift, but there has to be more. They do air magic in that class but never shows off. I wish I could help.*

Heading to history, Daisy knew that if the big personalities in that class were on display and in a fighting mood, things would get ugly, fast.

Chapter 4 - A Historic Lesson in Patience

Ember

Anger boiled within Ember as they headed to their second class of the day. They had to hold back their emotions or they may have lost control of the fire within them. If they could, they'd have headed out to a safe space and screamed, releasing a fireball into a brick wall or body of water. But no, it was time for Magical History. Thankfully, Felix and Daisy shared second period with them. Unfortunately, Josie had this class too, along with some of her posse.

I really don't like the popular crowd. This place would be much better if we could split it up into those here to learn and those here to be nasty.

Felix bumped his shoulder into Ember, finally catching up with them after their early retreat from class. "Are you okay?" His voice was low and full of concern. "You seem to be fuming there, my friend."

Ember squeezed their hands until their nails bit into their palms. They took a few deep breaths as they walked through the hall of the school, avoiding the other students. "I'm fine." Even Ember could hear the lie. If they could, they'd pause to talk, but there were too many students jostling their way to get to their final location.

Felix wrapped his arm around their waist. "Don't give Josie so much power. She doesn't deserve it. You pulled up dirt in class today. That was amazing."

Daisy scoffed. "I agree. She throws words at you like daggers. It's hard, but if you can ignore her, it'd be better."

"Hmm." Ember tried to hear their friends. "I just need a second to calm myself. I can't go in there and blow up at Josie, or worse, the other popular brats." *Or worse yet, blow them up.*

Though, imagining a few fireball-students did put a smile on Ember's face and relax a few muscles that had refused to unclench up until then.

The three of them reached their classroom. This was one of the few classes where they were assigned seats. Felix sat in front of Ember on the edge by the windows, but Daisy sat on the other side of the room. Previous year teachers warned each other that Ember and Daisy talked too much if they sat near each other. Despite disruptive talking, Josie and her friends always ended up near each other. They did sit in the front center, so that was something.

"Okay, everyone," Mr. Elias said when class began. "Pass your reports to the front of class." After the expected groans, he said, "You've known about this for a few weeks. It is due today, or it's a zero. I will not accept late work on this one."

Ember found their folder in their bag, pulled out the papers, and passed them up.

Ambrose, a beautiful girl with a slicked-back black ponytail, a black tank top, and short miniskirt who sat in the center front of the class, raised her hand. Everyone in class gazed at her. With her popularity, no one dared not. Even Josie basked in Ambrose's glory.

"Mr. Elias, is it true there's a resurgence of animosity against those who secured peace, those who worked with the shapeshifters? Rumor has it, the humans want to fight magic users because they fear us." She said that last as she smirked at Ember. "I've even heard a group wants witches to have more power ... because we do, you know, have more power. Humans *should* understand that. We live in peace by choice."

"This is ridiculous," Felix mumbled. He spoke up. "Just because we're born with abilities and powers other's don't have, doesn't mean we're better than them. Humans and witches have lived in peace for two hundred years. What's the point of this new uprising? Why would humans suddenly start fighting something that's working for them? The idea of this rumor is ridiculous. You know who's starting it, and it isn't the humans."

Ambrose smirked. "Such a simpleton, Felix. Aren't you smarter than this? Of course, it started with them. Can't you see that if we don't fight back now, the humans, who outnumber us, will get the upper hand?"

"He *is* dating Ember, so I would go with 'no' he isn't smarter. Or, he's a human lover." Josie laughed.

Felix rolled his eyes at Josie then turned back to Ambrose. "You're calling me 'simple' for understanding the balance of power around here? There's been peace since the war on that paper you wrote, or did one of your servants write it for you? Are you even *able* to do your own homework?"

Ember laughed behind their hands.

Back stiffening, Ambrose narrowed her eyes at him. "Just because my family has the power and prestige to have servants, doesn't mean you have to let your jealousy show."

"We all have power, Ambrose. The question is, are you smart enough to get the grades you get on your own." Felix sat back, eyes narrowing right back at the popular girl.

A paper ball hit Ember. Turning their head, they saw Josie's smirk. "Some of us have power. *Some* of us are just humans pretending to be witches taking up space in our school." Josie turned to Cress, a sandy-haired boy sitting next to Ambrose. "Have we figured out in three years what Ember's magical abilities are?"

The teacher cleared his throat. "The discourse is fine. Launching projectiles is not, Josie. One more and it's detention."

"Sorry, Mr. Elias." The smile on her face told everyone she was not at all contrite.

Cress gazed at the teacher, then at Ember, his hazel eyes narrowing. A single brow rose. "I've never seen them use magic of any significance."

"Again, Cress, keep it on topic." Mr. Elias looked ready to kick the trio of popular kids out of class. Ember couldn't agree more.

Gah, the three of them are a boil on this school. If only we could lance the wound and rid all of us of their arrogance. In the end, would anyone be saddened by their absence?

When Ember's family brought them to Feniks Secondary School, the administration demanded testing to prove Ember's abilities. It was considered standard that all witches have some proficiency in all practices of magic.

Ember hadn't shown their full extent of fire ability—it was better than most—and their parents had told them to hold back. It was all their father could do, all they had inherited from him. Even the small amount Ember showed was off the scales. The school had offered them some one-on-one lessons in private, and Ember and their parents thought they may learn some control and new spells, but it was quickly determined Ember outpaced even those who taught the skill.

Ember inherited air and spatial magic from their mom. The issue with Ember's air magic was, apparently it was rare in their grade. Only Daisy and one other kid shared that specialty. It was one of very few magic classes offered to multiple grades. Both eleventh and tenth shared the class. Ember did well in that class.

Spatial magic hadn't been tested or offered. Ember wasn't sure why. Maybe it was because it wasn't an elemental magic, though thaumaturgy and mind magic weren't elemental either. When they started, Ember was too intimidated to ask. Their mom had the training schedule at home, so they didn't worry, but over the years, Ember thought it odd that the school didn't include it as a topic of study.

Ember's mom's third proficiency was earth magic. Until now, Ember hadn't been able to do anything with soil.

One day, Ember would love to show their classmates their abilities in fire and spatial magic, but they'd spent their whole life hiding everything about themselves. Not even Daisy or Felix knew what they could do in those disciplines.

Until year nine when they'd been allowed to come to public school, Ember had always been homeschooled. Their whole life had been about hiding who they were. It was the first lesson their family had taught them. It was so ingrained, that now that they knew they could share parts of their life with their friends, they weren't sure when or how. After three years, Ember worried they'd feel hurt or betrayed at having been lied to.

Daisy's voice cut through their ruminations. "You saw Ember manipulate dirt today, Josie, you're just being a bully right now."

"Oh look, the guard dog speaks. Bark, bark, guard dog."

Mr. Elias moved to the center of the room. "That's enough, Josie. You know as well as everyone else that each student is tested before they are allowed to register at our school. Ember belongs here as much as anyone else, including you. When you're being mean ... maybe they belong even more. Just because Ember doesn't show off like most teens, doesn't mean they don't belong."

Wanting to change the subject, Ember raised their hand. Mr. Elias nodded. "Yes, Ember."

"Do you know why spatial magic isn't taught at the school?"

Josie, Ambrose, and Cress threw their heads back and laughed. A few other students snickered. Felix looked back at Ember, eyebrows coming together in concern.

They bit their lip, realizing they'd made another tactical mistake by asking the question.

Cress blurted out, "God above, they're simple as well as magically stunted. Spatial magic's a myth, you lout! Where *did* you come from before transferring here? Under a rock?"

Ember closed their eyes and waited for class to resume. *Just another day. These people don't matter in the larger scheme. You can make it ... just another day.*

It didn't take long for Mr. Elias's voice to carry over the din of student noise. "Ember, Cress isn't exactly correct that it's a myth, but we don't have time right now to discuss it. If you'd like, we can talk about it after school."

Everyone 'Ooo'd' as if Ember were in trouble.

Mr. Elias spent time on the lesson. With only a few minutes left, he said, "I know you're all very excited about ... well, everything teenager. But, we should discuss this weekend's field trip."

That got everyone's attention. The room finally quieted down, and focused on the idea of heading out to the woods for a few days.

Ember's stomach dropped. Whereas everyone else was excited, they dreaded the upcoming weekend. *What if I accidentally lose the permission slip? How mad would Mom and Dad really get?* They sighed, knowing it was a losing battle.

"As you know, we'll be leaving on Friday after lunch. We'll get to the site and split up. I'll have maps for each group so everyone can have their own area and no one will run into each other. You will be in groups of three. The back of the map has a list of the plants you should collect, pictures, and instructions on the process. You'll also have your phones so you can look up extra details or text me if you have any questions."

He checked over his notes. "I have a second list here. It explains what you need to pack and what the school will provide. There will be adults available to re-ice your cooler, help with fire, and help set up the school-provided tents. Most items you are required to bring yourself, so make sure you've looked over the supply list. Talk with your group, and plan accordingly."

Josie's hand shot up. "Yes, Josie?"

"Are you assigning the groups?"

The teacher flashed her a smile. "No. If you have to work together for that long, I suspect things will work better if you get to choose your own group. I would suggest you don't just go with your friends, though. This is an assignment with a grade."

She leaned back and smiled. "No worries, Mr. Elias. My friends *are* smart." She glared over her shoulder at Ember. "They have magic and brains, unlike some students in class."

She doesn't even know I can go yet. Ember winced just thinking about how excited Daisy would be. Their friend would have enough excitement for the both of them.

Mr. Elias sighed. "Don't push me, or I will assign the groups."

Josie sat up, looking stricken. "Sorry, Mr. Elias."

"I'm not the one you should be apologizing to."

She rolled her eyes, but the bell rang before she had to say anything more.

Chapter 5 - A New Voice in the Storm

Ember

As they filed out of class, Ember caught up with Daisy. "I'll see you in potions, fourth period."

Daisy gave them a quick hug. "You survived your first two classes. Josie must've woken up on the wrong side of her coffin this morning." They both laughed at this joke. "Things will get easier now ... it'll be a breeze."

Ember shook their head. "Can you imagine if vampires were real? Josie would totally fan-girl to become one."

Daisy snorted. "Totally."

After a wave, Ember headed down the hall with Felix to math class. The two were in Calculus BC. Being the only eleventh graders in the class, they didn't have to worry about the other students knowing about Ember's troubles with magic. Ember could go into class, learn, and leave.

They sat in the back corner. Felix turned to them. "Look, I know that you were homeschooled before coming here and you have some odd gaps in your knowledge. In other things, you're brilliant. Do you really not know about spatial magic?"

Ember just shrugged. They knew Felix wasn't trying to be condescending, but they really wished they could just forget about the last class.

"Cress is an idiot, but as Mr. Elias said, it isn't a myth. It is, however, like many things from the last war, believed extinct. It was always a scarce magic—only a few families had it—and it wasn't guaranteed to show up in kids. The witches who had it supported the phoenixes. They were deep behind enemy lines. None of them survived."

Ember's heart dropped. "None of them?" A boulder formed in their throat. They needed to speak to their mom about this.

Felix tracked the teacher walking to the desk, and they both knew class was about to start. "We can talk about this more later, but yeah, unless there is someone in hiding, that power is gone ... one more thing gone forever. Man, I hate war."

Ember couldn't agree more.

The teacher began speaking. Math was always one of their favorite classes, no opinions, no interpretation, just facts and correct answers. After fifty minutes of hard-and-fast note taking, Ember felt more grounded and ready to face their next class.

After the bell, Felix leaned in and kissed their cheek. "I'll see you at lunch."

Swinging their bag onto their back, Ember lumbered to potions class. They wished Felix were in that class as well, but he was in the advanced potions class. All of his classes were advanced. Ember's parents were correct when they said he was smart and good at what he did. Ember almost made it past the testing for that track but hadn't known all the plants and practices. Not in year nine. Now the regular-level class irritated them in how slow it moved ... except they enjoyed Daisy's company.

Entering the class, Ember sat next to their friend. Tables filled the room with cauldrons for mixing potions, burners, and trays with implements for cutting and scraping. Cupboards and shelves lined the walls, stuffed with ingredients and other potions paraphernalia. Each table could fit up to four students. Usually Ember had Daisy to themself. The potions teacher let the students choose their seats.

Before they could say anything, Simon, a small, quiet, nerdy student with mousey blond hair and blue eyes, slid into a seat at their table. He was in many of Ember's classes, including math and air magic. Despite their almost identical schedules, they rarely spoke.

Dropping his bag, he leaned in. "Did the two of you hear what Ambrose and the others were talking about in Magical History today?"

Ember groaned then searched their bag for their notebook.

Excitement oozed off Daisy. She was obviously happy to talk about the topic. "About the group that wants to fight back against the humans? I can't believe some of *them* want to subjugate *us*. Can you believe it?"

With a huff, Ember shook their head. "No, because it can't be true. It's lies and propaganda. Do you hear yourself right now? For over two hundred years, there has been peace. The humans and witches have lived and worked in concert with each other. Government, businesses, and, like, everything. There is no way that the humans have suddenly lost it to the point that they think fighting with magic users is a good idea." Ember wasn't sure why they were convinced of this, but they were. Though, unlike most of the students in the building, they had interacted with humans throughout their life. They needed to get home and do some research, talk to their parents, and jump on the internet.

Simon shook his head. "Really, Ember, don't prove Cress and the others correct. You have to be smarter than this. Why would anyone make this up? Of course it's real."

"Yeah, Ember!" Daisy jumped on the bandwagon, coming to Simon's defense. *Since when does she take his side?* "You remember the bad service we always get at the coffee shop? Not the humans, only us. It's a thing. You know it is. Not to mention, Simon wouldn't believe stories that weren't real. He isn't easily duped like *those* idiots." Those idiots being Ambrose, Cress, and Josie.

Ember bit their tongue, raised their eyebrows, then nodded. Daisy wasn't wrong about the local café, but they thought there was a different reason. In ninth grade, they were walking past the shop when the owner ran out saying they hadn't paid their bill. They hadn't been in the shop so they ran. Ever since, they'd been treated horribly.

In the end, Ember needed to get some facts before they could form a coherent argument.

Eyes sparkling with excitement, Simon leaned in a bit closer. "A group is forming on campus. There is an assembly meeting after school today. You two should come and learn more of the facts. I don't know if they'll meet again this week or next, but you can get your questions answered, get real information. You should come!"

Before Daisy could ask anything, the teacher interrupted them. "Today, we'll be taking a quiz on harvesting and storage of twenty of the most common plants we use in the potions we brew." She started handing papers out to each of them. "You each have your own quiz, so copying the person next to you won't help. Failing this quiz will mean you can't go on this weekend's field trip. A score less than eighty percent demands a redo."

The tall, elegant potions master glided around the room. Her green eyes took in everything as she handed out sheets of paper, her graying brown hair perfectly secured in a tight bun.

When the bell rang, Ember felt they'd done decently on the quiz. They'd been studying the fifty most common spell components for the last three years, so anyone not prepared had no excuse. They'd even handed in their permission slip with the quiz, securing their position on the weekend's trip. Though they were nervous about going, they did like the idea of hanging out with their friends for a few days.

As people started to file out, Ember waited. Daisy sat with them. "Did you think about what Simon said at all during the quiz?"

Ember considered the question. "Not really. Did you?"

"Oh my god, like, so much. I kept thinking about that meeting and learning about the group that's not letting the humans get one over on us."

"Do you really think that's what's happening?" Ember rubbed their temples.

"I don't know why you think this is a lie. You're usually smarter, Ember. Just come to this thing after school with me today, please. Listen to what they have to say, okay?"

"How about we go to lunch right now, and I'll think about it? I'm hungry."

Daisy shot up. "That sounds good too."

Ember stood more slowly. They weren't sure what it was about what Simon and the others said that didn't sit well with them. Maybe it was growing up with humans as friends and never having felt a real us-versus-them mentality.

Hopefully all this will blow over soon.

As much as Ember hoped, watching Daisy walk from the room, they worried their hopes weren't going to be answered.

Chapter 6 - A Little Here and a Whole Lot There

Felix

Felix left Ember and headed to his thaumaturgy magic lessons. Thaumaturgy was his weakest but probably his favorite magic. The idea of focusing magic on a small scale only to have it affect something larger in the bigger world intrigued him.

In mind magic, he held back in class. His father had taught him a lot, but he knew there were things the teachers could fill in. Though his dad knew some of the theories, he wasn't an educator, so he skipped over a lot Felix needed to know.

Earth magic was boring. The best thing about it was his friends. He knew Ember stressed out during the class, but it gave him an excuse to comfort them. If only Josie and Cress weren't in the class. The two of them had gotten worse and worse over the years.

He couldn't believe Cress had been his best friend when he was young. A cold shiver ran down his spine at the memory. His only excuse was they were young and Cress hadn't been as awful back then.

He worried about Ember. When he hung out at their house with their parents, they were relaxed, laughing and joking. He'd even seen Ember use magic. In school, they pulled it all in, hiding everything. He wasn't sure why.

In thaumaturgy class, he sat next to Lucy, an old friend. They'd been working together in this class and mind magic for years. They meshed well as class friends but not as well outside of school. Their other interests weren't compatible.

"How's your day going?" He asked, setting up for the day's lesson.

She looked up from a book, slowly closing it. He saw it was the latest from A.R. Grimes. He hadn't gotten that book and mentally put it on his list. "Good. Just inwardly preparing to spend a weekend with a bunch of teenagers."

"You do know you *are* a teenager, right?"

One of her brows popped up. "Only in the most technical of definitions."

He snorted. "Do you have a group?"

"Yeah. I'm all set."

The teacher interrupted them from continuing. "Okay, you each have a structure in the North Field and a model in the classroom. I'd like you to have a roof on your structure by the end of two weeks. This will take a bit of geometry to figure out. You may want to work with your partner or in a larger group. Let me know if you have any questions."

Gathering his small model, Felix looked it over. He'd constructed a basic cube so far. Everything on his tray should be exactly the same as what was in the field. They had camera feeds linked to their phones. He switched on the camera and checked it out. Sure enough, everything was as expected. He selected two 'beams' and 'dowels' and arranged them in a 'V' formation on his board, lying down for now what he wanted to be created out on his mat in the field. He closed his eyes, focused on what he created, and then pushed it towards his structure.

A wave of fatigue washed through him as the magic left him. This discipline took more from him than the rest. His breathing was rough, as if he'd just run a mile. He checked his phone and saw the pieces of lumber in the same orientation as on the small mock up in front of him.

He didn't think he could get the 'V' standing with his lowered magic resources, but he could make one more 'V.' That would be it for the day.

Finally completed, he dropped his head to his folded arms and let his body shake. It took a few minutes for the tremors to work their way through him. Once done, he moved the structure back to the shelves and waited. The teacher checked his phone and gave a single nod. "Grab a protein bar."

Most classes didn't provide any type of food, but this one tended to use more of the magical reserves than others. Students could unwittingly deplete themselves, so there were different options available to ensure students wouldn't collapse before the day was done. In the past, exactly that had happened.

Lucy chuckled. "Everyone in this school thinks you're invincible. They should see you after thirty minutes of this class. Rest, jelly boy. I'll grab you a bar, then you'll be fine by lunch. You can watch me finish my brilliant work."

He grunted. Lucy was brilliant in this area and seemed to have an endless reservoir of power.

"Hey, have you heard about this event after school today?"

He refused to lift his head. "What event?"

"I don't know. Something about a rally in the theater room. A group wanting to talk about the human-wizard uprising."

Felix lifted his head and glared at Lucy. "Please tell me you're kidding."

"Nope, not at all. The crazies are taking over the world!"

Chapter 7 - The Cat's Out of the Bag

Ember

The lunch room was full of noise and smells. Ember hated it. They hadn't brought lunch from home, so they got in line with Daisy. There were a few options, but the one the school messed up the least was pizza.

As they slowly shuffled forward, Daisy gushed about a movie she'd watched the night before. Ember half listened, focusing instead on getting through the line and to their table, away from the throngs of people. It was the one thing they struggled with adjusting to from being homeschooled ... crowds.

"If it isn't the dowdy twins." The voice sawed into Ember's ear from somewhere behind them. *Why can't I even have my downtime away from her?*

Ember slid their gaze back and saw Josie picking on Tansy and Olivia, two friends standing in line behind them. The two were also from grade eleven and were nice, quiet, and friendly. Perfect targets for the pariah, Josie.

Ember knew Olivia more than Tansy. They sometimes partnered in Magical Creations class together. Both were smart. Like Ember, they tried to stay out of the popular crowd's way.

Tansy, a bit taller than Olivia but still short with limp blonde hair and blue eyes, glared. "Go away, Josie. Learn to be happy without putting someone else down. When will you grow up?"

Olivia, brown hair covering her face, just shrank back.

Josie squawked and flipped her hair. "As if!"

Ember got to the front of the line and got their slice of pizza. *I should be more like Tansy. That was amazing.* Daisy followed, ordering fries and a bagel.

They slid through the throngs of students. Ember attempted to avoid the popular students as they found the table in the corner they normally occupied. Felix already sat with his lunch from home, sandwich in hand.

He took a sip of his soda as the two sat down. "Okay, this is important. The final groupings for this weekend's field trip need to be in by tomorrow morning. Ember, please tell me that you've finally convinced your parents to let you go. Did any of the campaigns we devise work?"

Guilt racked Ember as they thought of the lies they'd told their friends. They put the lack of the signed permission slip fully on their parents' shoulders. Truth be told, if it were just Felix and Daisy, Ember would love to go out and explore the woods. It sounded like something they'd done with their parents before moving to this area. But having the full eleventh grade class all tromping around the region, mostly unsupervised for over thirty-six hours ... they shuddered. Ember couldn't think of a less appealing thought.

Forcing a smile, they nodded at their boyfriend. "Yeah, they signed the paper last night. I gave my permission slip to Ms. Zwantry with my quiz. I should be good to go. The three of us can sign up after lunch."

Daisy pumped her fist in the air. "Yes! I knew you could do it." Thankfully, the cafeteria noise drowned out her exuberance.

A commotion from Josie and Cress had them all staring at the central table for a moment. Ember just shook their head before tucking in to eat.

Finally, Daisy dropped her shoulders. "Ember, why do you let the others get away with all their crap?"

"What do you mean?"

"We're in air magic class together. I know what you can do. I mean, you're not the best in the class, but you're not the worst. Why don't you just, I dunno, blow their homework on the floor every time they talk? Or better yet, mess up perfect Ambrose's hair?" Daisy's smile was wicked.

Ember snorted. "You know we aren't supposed to use our magic against other students."

Felix placed a hand on their knee. "What about fire? I know you don't attend any of the classes here, at least not the ones everyone else goes to, but that one day I was at your house and your dad asked you to light the stove. You just shot a laser beam, almost like an arrow, at the stove. I've never seen that kind of control. You sent *fire* at something that can explode, and neither of your parents blinked."

With a groan, Ember rubbed their temples. They forgot that Felix had seen that bit of fire magic. He was over enough that everyone forgot that Ember shouldn't do fire magic in front of him.

Daisy's jaw practically touched the table, and her eyes widened to the size of saucers. "You can do fire magic? Like, for reals? Fire *and* air? Why is this the first I'm hearing of this?"

Slanting a narrow-eyed glance at Felix, they turned to Daisy and shrugged. "I don't train here for my fire magic. I just do air and earth. To be honest, I don't need the other people to be impressed by me."

"But why not take classes? It doesn't make sense." Daisy was like a detective, sussing out a new story. She just wouldn't give this one up.

Ember sighed and massaged their forehead with one hand. There was no escaping this. "Felix is right. My fire magic is better than most of the others at the school. They can't really teach me much. Can we please just drop it and move on?"

"Like, students better or teachers better?" Daisy leaned in like this was the best gossip she'd heard all year.

Ember closed their eyes for a moment, assessing the piercing pain in their head. Was it real or psychosomatic because of the topic? "Look, this can't get out, but yeah, probably both. It's like this. You know my earth magic isn't great. It's like when I was born, instead of basic proficiency in all magic like you two have, maybe all magic users have, it was all put in fire with a splash of air mixed in for good measure."

"Whoa, so like, all your ability is just in fire magic?" Daisy sounded awed.

Ember bobbed their head left and right. "I guess ... more or less. That isn't exactly how it works, but it's a pretty good way to think about it."

Daisy slumped in her seat. "I don't get it, Ember. I'm your best friend. I've been to your house a million times, and you've been to my place. Why haven't you ever told me? I've never bragged about your air magic in front of the terrible three. You know I can keep a secret."

Guilt slammed into Ember at the hurt on their friends face. "At first I didn't tell anyone, and then, I don't know, it just didn't seem important."

"Right," Daisy said, voice flat. "But you could tell Felix, because he's so much more trustworthy?"

Ember took in a deep breath and let it out slowly. "I ... no. It wasn't like that. I think the time he saw me use the fire magic, we all forgot he was over studying."

Felix snorted. "Not to mention, I just assumed you knew. That's why I said anything in the first place. Of course, you'd know. You two are two peas in a pod."

A small smile formed on Daisy's face, and she sat a bit taller. "Yeah, okay." She ate a fry, and her eyes narrowed. "And before today you really thought spatial magic was still a thing?"

Ember snatched a French fry from their friend's tray and threw it at her. "Look, you, I've had just about enough out of you. It's hard to imagine a whole branch of magic dying off. If it happened to spatial magic, it could happen to one of the other disciplines, right? It's just crazy."

"Okay, fine," Daisy relented. "I guess that makes sense. So, did your parents name you Ember because they figured you'd only have fire magic?"

Ember snorted at the question.

Felix squeezed their knee. "At last, we're all better now. And this weekend we all get to go camping!"

Chapter 8 - That Would Be Masses With an 'M'

Ember

Ember stood outside the school, glad the day was over. Felix wrapped his arms around them and gave them a hug. "Lucy told me about this meeting after school. Are you really going with Daisy?"

They couldn't stop their eyes from rolling. "If nothing else, then to stop Daisy from completely falling for the propaganda. My head will be pounding by the end, I'm sure."

He leaned in and kissed them. "Do me a favor and take notes, even if just mental ones, and let me know later tonight about what they talked about."

"I was planning on brain dumping it all for the safety of my sanity, but if you're that interested, I guess. Then again, why not come with us? I'm sure it will be entertaining, if nothing else." Ember waggled their eyebrows to make their offer more enticing.

He rested his forehead on theirs. "As much as I would love to ... well, love to spend the time with you, I have a prior engagement I have to attend with my parents. I can't miss it. If there were any way out of it, you know I would. Even as awful as this sounds, it would be us together, and that is infinitely better than time not with you."

His words made Ember giddy. "I like spending time with you too."

"Enough of this, you two. You're in public. Break it up!" Daisy bounded down the school steps. "And Ember, we have a meeting to get to. You promised. We're going to be late!"

Ember pulled away from Felix and shifted their gaze to Daisy. "I did no such thing. I believe I said I *didn't* want to go to this farce. However, if you ask nicely, I'll go and try to behave."

"Don't promise the impossible," Felix mumbled next to them.

After a squeal of delight, Daisy asked, "Will you pretty please join me at this probably most excellent event?"

Ember shook their head at the ridiculous wording but smiled at Daisy. "Yes, let's go. I hear we're going to be late."

Daisy wrapped her hand around Ember's wrist and dragged them back into the school's theater. The room was packed, but they found seats in the back corner and watched the stage. Ember tried not to laugh at the irony of all this happening on a stage.

Ambrose popped out from the back, shortly followed by Cress. Ember waited for Josie, but the king and queen of popularity's main follower didn't appear. *Gods above, they're running this? Can it get any worse?*

Moving to the center of the stage, Ambrose bowed to the applause of the audience. She waved at a few friends and smiled. Then one of the stagehands gave her a microphone.

She tapped the end, and a loud scratch echoed through the room. Ember winced as the rest of the crowd quieted down. Moving the small wand near her mouth, she laughed the fakest laugh Ember had ever heard and said, "Oh, hi. I hope you can hear me."

A bunch of hands popped up, some with thumbs up. Ember fantasized about leaving ... or a giant fireball ... or using wind to cause havoc with the sound system. *Stop distracting yourself with things you won't do, and pay attention. How long can this vapid airhead talk, anyway?*

"Thank you for coming today. For those of you who don't know, if that is possible, I'm Ambrose, and this is my partner, Cress."

Ember couldn't help the eyeroll. *Oh yes, start with arrogance, brilliant Ambrose.*

"We are here to help you learn about a new movement. As all things new, it starts in the past, at the War of Peace." As she spoke, a magical shimmer took shape behind her.

Great, worse than a slide presentation ... a magical slide presentation.

As Ambrose spoke, the holograms depicted images of her words. "Back during the war when the Fighters for Peace and Unity fought Mages for Solidarity to keep them from subjugating humans, they didn't know part of the human agenda was to eradicate the 'others.' Have you ever contemplated why so many shapeshifters didn't survive the war? Well, history is always written by the winners, and the winning side had many magic users and just about all the shifters. But I'm not telling anyone anything they don't know. Am I right?"

The crowd erupted in cheers. Ember's gut clenched with the lies being consumed. Not only was this their history, so far she'd only brushed over the most known facts, warping the story into something new and horrible. Ambrose handed the microphone to Cress.

With his sandy-blond curly hair, hazel eyes, and athletic build, it was hard not to find him attractive, and he knew it. He used his allure to the best of his ability as he sauntered to the front of the stage.

"As the beautiful Ambrose said, there were two parties fighting, and the winning side had the shifters. For two hundred years, we've lived in peace with the humans, but at what cost? What have we lost? What did they gain? In the end, was it worth it?"

The crowd yelled, "No!"

"We lost the werepanthers. Was *that* worth it?"

"No!"

"We lost some of our magical abilities. Was *that* worth it?"

"No!"

"We lost our phoenixes. Was *that* worth it?"

"No!"

At this point, all the students sitting in the seats were bouncing and yelling, completely riled up by what Cress said.

He continued. "There are other shifters, some still alive, but they are few, far between, and rarely seen. And while our magical community hasn't shrunk, we've stayed stagnant in our size. At the same time, the human community has grown, and the humans feel that they are more powerful than us, that *they* have the right to subjugate us!"

The crowd went wild, leaping up from the seats, yelling in agreement, whooping and cheering. While Daisy sat next to Ember, observing the excitement, Ember tried to keep a neutral face.

How are any of these people taking any of this for real? Humans are our neighbors, live all around us, and, in many cases, are our friends. Has everyone so quickly forgotten?

It took time before the two speakers could continue. Ember took that time to think about what they'd heard. Nothing of the early stuff was incorrect, but the way they spun it. Two hundred years ago, the majority of magic users agreed that keeping the peace with the humans, creating a world where everyone worked and lived as equals, was the right decision. The small group that didn't agree got overthrown. *This group is making it sound like most magic users still feel the hurt of living and working with humans.*

Ember muttered low, though with the boisterous crowd, they could've yelled their displeasure. "I've never trusted a word Ambrose or her cronies have said, and why should I start now?"

When Ember focused on the stage again, Ambrose had the microphone. "In the next few weeks, it will be our job to remind the humans that they are not equal to us.

We can do what they cannot. They need to respect us and let us lead them before it's too late."

Ember jerked their head as if slapped. "Too late for what? Just because we have abilities doesn't make us smarter or better leaders. What is she talking about?"

Daisy leaned forward in her seat, barely still sitting in it. She swung her hand back and swatted Ember's arm. "Hush. I want to hear this. This is the smartest I've ever heard Ambrose speak."

Well, it wouldn't take much to be her smartest speech ...

Cress had the microphone again. "I have worked with and for both humans and wizards, and trust me, the humans resent us, I know. If we don't take a stand now, they will. They'll work to make *us second-class* citizens. *That* is their end goal, *that* is their hope and dream, *that* is what we must worry about. "

The reaction from the crowd was deafening. The students around them stomped their feet and cheered.

Smiling wide, Cress stepped to the edge of the stage. "There is already legislation in the works to ban magic from some areas, and magic users if they can tell us apart. They want to label us, like in *The Scarlet Letter.* Well, I for one say, 'no!' That is never going to happen to me! I refuse to allow them to make me a second-class citizen. Ambrose and I are here today, standing on this stage, hoping all of you will hear us, believe us, and help us protect our own. Do *you* refuse to become a second-class citizen too?"

Chapter 9 - A Star Is Born

Ambrose

"**A**s you can see, we may be fewer in number but we allowed the humans their time to shine and equality, and they've taken that as an invitation to try to step beyond their stations. Currently the political structure in the nation is biased towards the humans, since there are more of them than us, and they use that to bend the laws, their laws, in favor of anti-magic policies, but that has got to stop."

Ambrose waited for the cheers to sink in. Standing taller, she breathed in their adoration. The auditorium was full of students from every grade. Before, she was popular in her grade. Now, everyone would love her.

Their love fed her body and soul, making her feel larger than life. She lived to be in the spotlight. She didn't care about any of this. When her dad asked her to run this assembly, she jumped at the idea to increase her presence in the school. *I'm going to be the most popular person in the history of this place. They'll name a wing after me!*

The wizard, Tad Shade, had come to her family with an idea, one that would bring the magic users more power. Her family had power, but they could always use more. They would become the new leaders. *And I would be the face of the movement. Who else, really? I'm young, beautiful, and popular.*

"Ambrose," her father had said, voice stern. "We have a proposition for you."

She sat in her room fixing her makeup for dinner. Her father coming to her at such times wasn't unheard of, especially when he wanted something. "What is it, Father?"

"Power. A way to get more power."

The crescendo started to dissipate. She brought the microphone back to her mouth. Cress stood by her side, handsome and tall and dumb enough to not know when he was being used. "We will show the humans who have decided they are better than us that they have thwarted the wrong group. If you want to play with fire"—she created a fireball eight inches in diameter hovering above her left hand—"you will get burned."

As the crowd went wild, she and Cress smiled and waved. She dissipated the fireball, and after another minute, they headed backstage. Josie waited for them out of sight of the crowd. The girl was useful. Always following them, reminding everyone that they were the power couple on campus.

Josie's green eyes sparkled. "You two were great! That was amazing. Everyone here will go home, convince their parents that what you said was brilliant, and bam! The movement has begun in earnest. No more seedy websites. Now it'll be legit."

Cress pulled Ambrose in for a kiss. She gave him a moment before pulling away. "You're right. We have done what neither Mr. Shade nor my dad could've done. We've made this movement real. Did you arrange for the fliers to be handed out?"

Josie smiled. "I got some nerds to create a website during lunch and print out fliers with information about another event next week. He and his friends are handing them out as people leave. They'll create posters we can hang on the walls as well."

Cress purred, "Good job, Josie. You're a treasure."

The girl preened. She was so easy to manipulate.

Ambrose smiled at her. "Can you monitor everything here? Cress wanted to take me out to dinner tonight to celebrate."

His brows came together for a moment of confusion before he nodded. "That I did."

Josie's smile widened. "Yes! You two should celebrate. I'll make sure everything here gets completed." She spun and left.

Cress leaned down and whispered in Ambrose's ear. "One day, she's going to say no to you, love."

Ambrose smiled. *Maybe, but today is not that day.*

Chapter 10 - Decompressing

Ember

Outside of the school, Ember gave Daisy a quick hug. "I'll see you tomorrow."

"Thanks for coming with me. It was so interesting. I wonder if I can find anything online." She looked at the flier that had been handed out as they shuffled through the door. "Oh my gods! Yes! Look at this. Not only is there a website, there's another info session next week on Thursday. This is amazing. Will you go with me again?"

Blowing out a large breath, Ember slowly bobbed their head. "Let's survive this weekend first." Cold dread flowed through them now that the deed of handing in the permission slip was done. *No getting out of it now!*

"What do you mean, 'survive this weekend'? Collecting night ingredients from Bishop Bay Forest is simple. I spent half my childhood playing in those woods."

Ember rubbed their eyes. "Again, *you* did. I'm more of a city person. I don't know enough of the dangers lurking behind each of those scary trees."

"There *are* no dangers. If there were, the school wouldn't send students out there, mostly alone, every year."

"Fine, you're right. This is a yearly event, and it isn't like the school has an accepted number of student losses it allows for. Okay, no more worrying." Ember gave Daisy a wan smile before turning and heading home.

They pulled out their phone and sent a text to Felix. Info session interesting or maybe terrifying, depending on point of view. Another one next week. Beyond the horribly terrifying message, guess who ran it?

Closing the phone, they focused on the walk home. A vibration in their hand let them know a reply had come.

Talk after dinner? I'd love to hear about the meeting. Who led it?

A warmth bubbled in Ember's belly, warming the fear for this weekend, and they smiled. You'll just have to wait until after dinner. Anticipation is good for you.

Felix sent an eye roll emoji and a heart blowing emoji.

At home, Mom had prepared lasagna and a salad. They dropped their bag by the stairs and sat at the table.

Dad sipped his wine. "You're home awfully late today. Something interesting happen at school, or did you and your friends just get caught up in talking?"

Ember huffed out a laugh then rolled their eyes. They handed the flier to their dad. "There was this info session held after school. Daisy really wanted to go and wanted me there too. It was ... well, awful. Not only did Ambrose and Cress run the meeting, I couldn't believe the crap they spewed. Mom, Dad, have you heard about this? It's like this group wants to restart the War of Peace, but they crave a different ending. And without the shifters, who will stop them?"

Mom brought the food to the table and sat. "Did they say why they want to start things up again?"

"They're rewriting history, saying there were a lot of magic users, a majority even, who didn't want an ending to the war where humans and witches lived as equals. This group is implying peace was forced on us. Moreover, they're saying the *humans* are bristling at the current arrangement, too, and starting to fight. All the animosity, apparently, started with them. The humans are jealous of our superior power."

As Ember spoke, both their parent's faces hardened.

"You know, we lost good people in that war, and not so these upstarts could ignore the outcome. Who do they think they are?" Dad's anger filled the room.

Mom sighed. "Ember, dear, it's good to know what went on during that rally. You shouldn't let yourself become ignorant of the world around you. I fear your dad and I may have done that in the last ... well, bit of time. We've been focused on raising you. As always, keep that head of yours thinking, keep your opinions safe, and especially, keep yourself safe."

"What about my friends?"

Dad grunted. "Talk to Felix. He knows what's going on and has a good head on his shoulders. I can't see him falling for that drivel. You said Daisy attended with you and wants to go again? She seemed taken in by what she heard? Be careful. People can be easily swayed by propaganda. Friendships can be lost. I just—"

Mom put a hand on Dad's forearm. "What Dad's trying to say is, for now, until we know how big this is, keep your opinions to yourself. Like your magic, it isn't anyone's business but your own. If you feel it's easier to go with Daisy to this rally, then go, but if you need an excuse, tell her we need you here."

After dinner, Ember headed to their room and called Felix. He was of the same opinion as their parents. "If you want to go to that meeting next week with Daisy, I'll join you two. I don't like the sound of what those two said. I'm sure it's Ambrose running the show. Her or someone in or attached to her family."

"What about Daisy?"

Felix huffed. "She's smart, but naive. You said she's going to go home and look things up. I know she loves social media, but in the end, she's good at research. Look at her grades. Give her time to figure things out. My guess is she'll see through this in the end."

A lump formed in Ember's gut. "I don't want to lose her. Dad talked about this type of thing breaking up friendships. She was my first real friend ... pretty much ever."

"I know." Felix's voice came over the line, soft and comforting. "I really think we should trust her ... *you* should trust her."

"Felix, you didn't see the crowd and what Ambrose and Cress did to everyone. It was like I was in the twilight zone. It was bonkers."

"Hopefully this weekend will help to ground people, remind them that they know non-magic users. This movement is new and dumb. The people running it are probably after something else. Just look at them. It's all ridiculous. You know that, right?"

"I do. Don't worry. I know it has to be some magic user stirring up trouble. I just don't understand why. What is the point of all this?"

His voice sounded strained. "Good questions. Mine is who? Who is behind all of this?"

Chapter 11 - A Breeze Blows In

Ember

Ember and Daisy headed to air magic class. First period swapped between magical disciplines. Earth magic met on Mondays and Wednesdays. Air magic met Tuesdays and Thursdays. Fridays, they had a study hall. The class was on the top floor of the school.

Ember and Daisy trudged up the stairs early Thursday morning.

"I'm so tired," Daisy moaned. "Why do we always have to traverse all these steps?"

Ember laughed. "We need access to the sky, my friend. It would be hard to do that from lower down in the building, don't you think?"

"Fine, be logical. See if I care?"

Unlike earth magic, air magic met indoors, but the roof of the room could open to the sky. The class met in a top-floor classroom almost the size of a gymnasium. This allowed the students room to spread out. Despite the size of the space, the only eleventh year students were Daisy, Ember, and Simon. There weren't any other eleventh years with this proficiency, not at either the basic level nor the advanced level. There were a few tenth year students in the class with them so they'd have more people to learn with. Both the ninth and twelfth year classes were full.

They both threw their bags by the wall and sat waiting for the rest of class to fill in. Ember liked this class. Though they kind of knew the other students a bit, they didn't know them well.

Mrs. Vintl came out of her office. She was one of the youngest instructors Ember had, probably in her late twenties or early thirties. She had short blonde hair and gray eyes. She may have been the only person on campus that could compete with Daisy for energy levels. "Okay, students, create a small twister on your color. Follow the lines on the floor. Choose the challenge line you feel up to."

Ember debated as they created a twister on the green dot that had been assigned to them. Each person had their own color and lines to follow. They decided to take the straight line, though some of the other lines looked more interesting.

Before they came to Feniks Secondary School, Ember had sat down with their parents and discussed magic. There were some areas where they flourished, like air and fire magic, and others where they were hopeless ... almost everything else. In the agreement to join public school and meet new people, Ember knew they had to hide in plain sight, blend. If they were too splashy, they feared their family would end up moving again.

They remembered telling their parents, *"Don't worry. I'm going to hold back, be invisible. I want to learn the basics anyway. Most of what I do seems pretty natural, so if I can get the building blocks, it can only help, right? And maybe I'll make a friend along the way."*

Ember's dad had smiled. "Knowledge is never a bad thing, kiddo."

Once Ember's twister was across the room, they heard the phone ring in Mrs. Vintl's office. Everyone was focused on their own task. Ember saw Daisy's twister on its red path halfway across the floor. Knowing they had time, Ember started over and took the hardest path. *No one will see me, anyway. I can stretch my magic and stay unseen.*

The winding zig-zag path was fun. Ember focused on getting their twister through the intricate pattern before anyone noticed what they'd done. They took one turn too quickly, and their spiral of air almost jumped onto Simon's path, but they held on tight to their magic, forcing their twister to do their bidding.

In the background, Ember heard Mrs. Vintl wrapping up her phone call. Heart beating faster, they wanted to get to the end. They lifted their hands, rotating and turning both fingers and palms, forcing their magic to their will. In the end, their twister crossed the line just as they heard their teacher signing off.

They huffed out a small laugh.

"You did it, Ember. Good for you!" Daisy beamed up at them. "Which of the three paths did you take?"

The easy and the hard one? "Um, the middle one."

"Oh! Me too. It was tricky in the middle, but fun, no?" Daisy's earnest look had Ember nodding. They didn't have a better answer anyway.

Simon sauntered over. "I did the hard one today. Maybe someday you'll be up to my level. It takes skill, practice, and focus. I know that sounds like a lot of work, but it's worth it. You just have to decide to spend less time on social media and more time on your studies."

Ember bit the inside of their cheek. Grades were never revealed to the class, but often teachers told the class the range of scores. They knew they were always near the top. Simon had no problem letting everyone know when he scored the top grade. When it wasn't him, he was usually in the top three or four. He never asked who the other top scores belonged to.

I wonder if it'd surprise him if he knew me and Daisy were two of his toughest competitors. Add Felix, and we're the ones forcing him to study more. Tansy and Olivia probably make up the last of the truly brainy brainiacs. The last two are the only ones he probably knows about. So stuck in his own head.

"Alright, class. We're going to create balls of air and play catch. The balls should look like a ball but not blow papers around. We'll start with throwing the ball today and move up to having papers out next week."

Ember and Daisy moved to the side of the room together.

Mrs. Vintl continued to speak. "You can be in groups of two or three. One person should create the ball, but when the ball gets to the apex, control of the sphere should shift."

Simon came up to them. "Can I join your group?"

Ember opened their mouth to say no, but Daisy said, "Sure. Why not."

"I'll make the initial ball," Simon said. "That way we know, at least at the start of this, we'll have a good grade."

The words felt like daggers to Ember. In the end, they really didn't care about their daily grade. Ember knew they could make it up as this lesson continued. They just wanted to wipe that smirk off Simon's face. "Sure, whatever."

The three separated, and Simon made a ball. Behind their back, Ember flicked their fingers, and the ball dissipated.

He tried again, and Ember pushed the tiniest bit of their magic. After his third attempt, Ember cleared their throat. "Maybe we should let Daisy make the ball."

Face scrunched up in frustration, Simon shook his head. "Yeah, fine. Whatever."

Eyes wide, Daisy created a ball and threw it to Ember. They caught it at the top of the arc and brought the ball close to their hands. Then they threw the ball to Simon. Ember felt when he took over control and let him take it. On the second round, Ember unwound Simon's magic when the ball was half way to Daisy.

They saw Mrs. Vintl approaching, so they decided to stop messing with Simon. He practically had steam coming from his ears.

"I don't know what's happening to me today," he mumbled.

When the teacher got to their group, they did two rounds without much of a hitch. "Very good, you three. You look ready for the next step. I'm proud of you."

As she moved on, Ember messed with Simon one more time.

"For goodness sakes," he stammered. "What is wrong with me?"

Ember sat in their room, deciding on what to pack for a weekend in the woods. They wanted warm and sturdy. They knew with the need of night plants they wouldn't be getting much sleep the first night, but that didn't mean they couldn't wear comfortable clothing.

As they searched for worn jeans and sweatpants, their phone rang. After a quick check of the display, they answered. "Hiya, Daisy."

"Hi, Ember. Are you ready for tomorrow? I'm super excited."

"Getting there. I have the list school provided, and I'm debating what more we'll need."

A sound suspiciously like Daisy flopping on her bed came over the line. "I packed earlier this week. Most of what I'll wear isn't the same as what I wear to school, so it was pretty easy. Don't forget washcloths for cleaning and deodorant."

Snorting, Ember found the items and threw them in their duffle bag. "Anything else?"

"Yeah, class was weird today, don't you think?"

"You'll have to be more specific, my friend. I have more than one a day." Ember continued circling their room, gathering items for the field trip.

"Simon had so much trouble with air magic. He's usually so much better. I wonder what that was all about. Any ideas?"

"Look, he's arrogant. Don't let his over-inflated opinion about himself color your opinion about him. We, as a group, did fine. It's like that assembly thing on Monday. It spoke well of itself, but when you dig deeper …."

Daisy scoffed. "You promised to give it a chance. I'm doing more research, but it's taking time. Between homework and this field trip, I don't have a lot of free time, but I will be doing a deeper internet dive next week. As for you, don't just ignore the message because it comes from the terrible trio, okay?"

Ember sighed. That wasn't what they were doing … at least it wasn't what they thought they were doing. "Fine, deal. Now, I'm going to go. You're too distracting to talk to while I pack. I'll end up with fourteen shirts and no pants."

Daisy laughed as they got off the phone with each other.

Chapter 12 - And So It Begins

Ember

Ember sat at the lunch table with Felix and Daisy on Friday. Their friends were talking about the school field trip. The more Felix and Daisy's excitement grew about heading out once the meal finished, the more Ember's apprehension solidified. *Why did I agree to do this?*

Daisy practically vibrated in her seat. "Can you believe it? We miss gym and English ... and half our classes! And then we get to be in school all weekend. This will be fantastic!"

Ember smiled at their friend. "You'd be more convincing that you wanted to miss class if you didn't end with your excitement over a weekend of school."

"Fact." Felix laughed. "But I agree with Daisy on this. The weekend will be amazing." His eyes lit up with his anticipation as he looked between Ember and Daisy, holding his sandwich in his hand halfway to his mouth. "Did you each follow the list of things to bring? I don't want to find out tomorrow night we need something."

"Yes, Daddy." Daisy made a face at him, shaking her head. "You texted the split-up list of what each of us should bring from the school guide of food and supplies. Now, did you get what I sent on *my* list?"

He snorted. "Yes, I got marshmallows, chocolate, and graham crackers. I assume you assigned sweets to each of us?"

Finally, happiness bubbled in Ember at their friend's antics. "I have the sandwich cookies and frosting."

At each sweet, Daisy's eyes grew. "This will be epic. Okay, I brought milk, chocolate milk, and soda. It's all in the cooler. We should be set."

"I also brought some non-sugary foods. I hope you two did as well." Ember gazed back and forth at the others.

"We're going to be out there until Sunday morning. I can't live on sweets alone."

Daisy's jaw dropped. "What? You're a teen. Of course you can!"

Felix raised his hands, shrugging. "Only time will tell."

Mr. Elias came into the cafeteria. "Eleventh years, it's time to go. Grab your bags, and meet out by the buses."

Ember stood with a gaggle of other students. There were just under sixty students heading out to the woods, about twenty groups going out to harvest moonlight plants.

The school had chartered three buses. Each bus could hold thirty people. There were adult volunteers who would help monitor the students, but it would be hard to be everywhere during the three days and two nights.

Daisy dragged Ember to a seat near the center of one of the buses. Felix sat across from them. Simon ambled onto the bus, and sat next to him. Apparently, he had no one else to sit with. Felix turned to Simon. "Who are you partnering with?"

Simon had been gazing out the window. He flopped back onto his seat and turned to Felix. His voice carried across the aisle to Ember. "Olivia and Tansy. They needed someone, and they're almost as smart as me."

The bus jerked and began to roll. The park was close, so the ride wouldn't be long. Ember watched the neighborhood homes slide by behind Felix's head then focused on Simon. His arrogance always baffled them.

Why Olivia and Tansy relented to work with him was beyond them. Ember wouldn't have wanted to spend that much time with his bossiness.

"Is that your only criteria?" Felix asked, pulling Ember out of their musings.

"Isn't it yours? What other qualification would you want in a school assignment? You usually partner with Ember, and they're smart. Isn't that why you two always work together? Then again, you are also partnering with Daisy, but she and Ember are probably a package deal."

A laugh exploded out of Daisy next to the window. Looking over at her, Ember saw her slap her hands over her mouth as she shook her head. She hadn't shifted her gaze from her phone, so it could've been something from there, but Ember doubted it.

Swiveling back to Simon and Felix, Ember saw Felix's chest rise and fall in a deep sigh. "On an assignment that goes this long, were you at all worried about compatibility of personalities?"

Simon's left shoulder jerked up and down. "I don't really care much about socialization. We just need to get in and out and be on our way. Get some ingredients tonight that require immediate boiling and then tomorrow night's plants that can be grabbed and stored. It's relatively simple."

A loud screech and jerk came from the front of the bus, and the bus came to a stop. Ms. Zwantry, the teacher on their bus, stood. "Okay, everyone, make sure you take a map of the area each group was assigned. Gather your bags, school-supplied tents—two per group—and your group members, and locate your campsite. If you aren't sure where to go, one of the adults will help you find the location. Once you get settled, make sure your tents are set up and you have your food stored properly. Expect a checkup in the next hour and a half to two hours. As long as we are out here, there are a few regular ingredients you can collect on top of the night plants. That should be done tomorrow during the day."

As they headed to their campsite, Felix touched Ember's forearm. "I don't know how much you've heard about this field trip—it isn't talked about much in the secondary school—but the lower grades talk about it a lot. I guess older siblings tell their kid siblings about it and then it's gossiped about when we're younger. Anyway, pranks are the name of the game."

Ember paused, a cold chill making them shiver. "Pranks?"

Daisy bounced. "Well, yeah, of course, but don't worry. It isn't like we have to do any. And if we're diligent, we shouldn't have to worry. We'll get our plants, make our s'mores, and nothing will happen. Again, this weekend will be epic!"

Mouth dry, it took a few seconds for Ember to get their feet to start moving again. They tried to lick their lips, but they suddenly wished they'd been more adamant about saying 'no' to this. Ember gazed over at Ambrose, Cress, and Josie, the trio from hell, all devious smiles. The three spent as much time searching the faces of the other groups as gathering their stuff. *Those three are going to be a problem.*

It took twenty minutes of trekking the paths to get to their campsite. They had two tents—one for Daisy and Ember, one for Felix. The three worked together to get everything set up.

Once done, Ember took a moment to stretch their back. They couldn't see or hear any of the other students. They knew from the map where they were located, but the school had done a good job of giving everyone enough space to work with their group, alone.

Ember and Daisy found a couple of logs that could work as seats. Using a bit of wind to lessen the weight, they moved the logs to where they wanted to make a fire pit. After setting up the seating, Daisy headed off to sort the tent while Felix headed to the lake for water. Ember looked around them to make sure they were alone, then flicked their fingers, and a fire blossomed to life.

When Daisy returned, she gaped. "Did you do that? I don't see any matches or anything." Her head swung around as she searched the woods, then her voice dropped. "Did you use magic?"

Not used to anyone making a big deal of it, Ember jerked their head up and down once.

Daisy covered her mouth to stop any sound of excitement. "And now we have fire. How easy *is* that for you?"

Ember bit their lower lip. "Yeah, not that hard." They felt their face heat with embarrassment.

Felix returned, and they started to heat the water for chocolate milk. Daisy encouraged Ember to fill him in on what they'd done magically.

One of the parent volunteers came into the site and checked off that they passed inspection. "You three are good to go. You may want to get some rest. You'll be heading out just after eleven to find the night time plants. You'll need to boil the roots. The liquid needs to be collected, as well as the roots, stems, and leaves. Everything needs to be in containers before four a.m., when the sun starts to show. Don't forget the list of tomorrow's plants, both day and night."

The three nodded. Once the adult left, Daisy dove into the bags to find food. "We're having s'mores, and then we can rest. We can get up at ten for real food."

No one argued with her plan.

Chapter 13 - Mind Over Matter

Ember

Ember smelled something meaty cooking. They stretched and kicked their sleeping bag. Rolling to their back, they pushed up to a sitting position. The tent was empty. The air temperature had cooled in the few hours they'd napped. They searched their bag for a sweatshirt and slipped it on. Shoes next, and they headed to the fire.

Both Daisy and Felix were already up. As they sat down beside Felix, he handed them a metal poker and a hot dog. "Welcome to Cafe Bishop Bay. On the menu tonight are our best hot dogs flambé. Enjoy." Daisy laughed, and Ember gave him a tired smile.

They each ate a couple of dogs before setting up to search. A flashlight, a sack on their back with a small shovel, hardy scissors, some storage bags, and hard case storage boxes. Daisy carried the images of the plants they needed to find, though they'd studied them so much, they probably had them all memorized. A side pocket held gloves.

It took them hiking and searching most of an hour to find the first of the three plants they needed. Thankfully, it was the plant with the most complicated storage procedure. Of the three plants they had to find, the root of this plant required the most time to simmer, low and slow. They each harvested some of the flowers, leaves, stem, and root.

Daisy held the parts of the plant. "I could head back to camp and start boiling the root. The other two don't need as much time, and I don't want to mess this up."

Ember bit their lip but nodded. No one outside their family knew this, but their eyesight was good, better than most humans or witches, even in only the moonlight.

Felix shrugged. "It's one of the reasons there are three of us. That sounds good. Head back. We'll find the other two plants. Do you know the way?"

"Sure do! I know these woods like the back of my hand." She swung around and headed back in the direction they'd come.

The next plant didn't take any time at all. Felix had the small shovel out when Ember heard Daisy call.

Ember swung their head around in the direction they heard the yell. "Did you hear that?"

Felix shook his head. "Hear what?"

"Daisy. She yelled for us. She sounded ... she needs us."

Another scream. This one sounded like Daisy was in pain.

"Felix, you had to have heard that. She's hurt. We have to go. This is more important than a grade."

Felix put his hand on Ember's shin. "There wasn't any sound. Listen to me—"

Terror gripped Ember. Felix wasn't listening to them. "Why aren't you worried? It's Daisy. She's in trouble, in pain. Why don't I go after her, help her." Anger began to boil in them. "If you're that worried about the stupid plant, stay. I'm going to go to help my friend."

"Ember, wait!"

Ember pulled away and snapped, "You can stay here."

Anger overwhelmed Ember. What was wrong with Felix? Were his grades that important to him? Was he really going to just ignore a friend in need?

"Ember! Help! Oh my gods! It hurts!"

Daisy's voice rang out. Ember ran. Their heart pounded as the trees streamed past them, blurs of dark green. A few branches reached out to scratch them, like hands trying to grab them. The woods took on a cartoon quality of a repeating background, everything blurry and repeating.

It didn't take long for Ember to realize they didn't know which way to go. They turned in the direction they thought Daisy's voice came from, but they weren't sure. *Where am I? Where is Daisy?* Pausing, they spun.

"Ember!"

They whipped around towards Daisy's voice. Once they had a direction to go, they ran. The land around them became a haze of leaves and twigs. Branches scraped their arms and face. Warmth on their face told them one of the scratches may have been bleeding.

A tree reached out—*is that a snarl?*—and snagged Ember. With a jerk, they heard a rip, and they were free. Their lungs burned as they darted towards their friend, terror surging through them. Every now and then a whimper let them know their running was on target.

Is she okay? What is wrong with her? Will I be able to help her? What happened to her? Are there deadly animals in these woods that the school officials just didn't know about? Gods, will I be fast enough?

Worse and worse scenarios played out in their mind.

It was so dark, Ember could barely see. Their eyesight was better than most people, but with the trees blocking off the moon, it was almost impossible to see where they ran. They kept stumbling. Their vision darkened. Suddenly, they ended up on their hands and knees. A sharp pain radiated up their right leg.

They panted, lying on the ground. Their leg hurt, but Daisy's voice came to them again. *"Ember, help me!"*

Groaning, Ember pushed to their feet. The pain in the leg made them flinch, but they had to get to Daisy, but where was she? Did they overshoot where she was? Miss a turn? They limped in a circle until they thought they heard a whimper. Then they made their way in the direction they thought they'd find their friend.

Ember made it another few steps then leaned against a tree. The pain in their leg brought them to tears. They realized their body trembled, and they couldn't imagine putting more weight on their foot. Their tears burned their cheeks, and their gut twisted as they thought about Daisy.

What happened to her? Is she okay? Why can't I hear her anymore? Is she too far gone to call out to me? Oh my gods, is she okay? Please, Hestia, keep her safe at our hearth. Please, Artemis, keep her safe in our woods.

Ember slid down, collapsing into themself, realizing they'd never get to Daisy. A lump of hate and doubt threatened to crush them. Breathing became a struggle.

A hand landed on their head, and a coolness washed through their mind. They shivered, as it felt like a war battled in their mind. *What is happening?* Their body jerked, and they slammed against the tree. A low moan escaped them.

Felix's voice flowed over them. "It'll be fine, trust me. This has to be Cress. He's throwing images into your mind, manipulating you. It's almost impossible to track, but I can protect you ... but you need to relax and trust me. This is a mind attack. I didn't expect this when I warned you about pranks."

Ember couldn't speak. They groaned, leaning harder into the tree. The sharp bark bit into their back.

After a few hours? Days? Years? Felix rubbed down their head to their side. "I think I got him out of your mind. How do you feel?"

"Umm." They shook their head. "My head hurts. What did he do to me?"

"He put a suggestion into your mind and kept layering it with more details. First that Daisy was hurt? I'm guessing he just threw directions at you, keeping you running. Is your leg okay?"

They reached down and rubbed from their knee down. "I think I twisted my ankle. It really hurts. Walking tomorrow is going to suck. Walking now won't be much better. And we have to go back for that plant and one more. Gah, I really don't like him, or them."

Felix stood, then carefully helped Ember up. "Okay, speedy. I got the second plant. I had already pulled it when you began to freak out. Let's head back to camp and get you watching the boiling roots. Daisy and I can head out for the last one."

It took them forty-five minutes to get back to camp, and when they did, Ember felt ready to pass out. Their head hurt, their ankle hurt, and their body felt weak.

When Daisy heard about what happened, she wanted to find Cress and open up a wet mud pit under his feet. The idea he'd mess with Ember's mind went beyond basic pranks. It took both Ember and Felix to convince her it was better to not go after the trio of popular evil.

Ember sat by the fire and stirred every twenty minutes as the other two headed out. *Why did I agree to do this?*

Between stirring, Ember grabbed a bandage Daisy left near them and wrapped their ankle. It hurt, but they knew it would be better by morning. Their healing was good, better than most in the magical world. It would be sore, but they'd be able to walk. They found some water and waited for the other two to return. With a small push of magic, they called their bag to the firepit. They knew spatial magic was supposed to be extinct, so they made sure to be more careful with that magic than any of the others.

Ember dug around until they found a painkiller and hoped it would help with the pounding in their head. They'd never had anyone attack them with mind magic. When they got home on Sunday, they'd have to ask their parents. There must be something they could do to protect themselves.

Chapter 14 - A Plan

Ambrose

Ambrose and Cress watched as Felix led Ember off, the human-playing-witch limping. Ember didn't seem to have magic. Ambrose had no idea why they were part of the school or on this trip. Moreover, before Ember came, Felix was part of their crew, *her* crew. He was always nice, but she and her family had been working on him. She was sure by ninth or tenth year, he'd be putty in her hands. He'd have been a better match for her than Cress, the half-wit.

It hadn't taken Felix more than a few minutes to break Cress's hold on Ember's mind. What use was it dating a mind wizard if any other magic user could figure out his spell and unravel it so easily? If she could show Felix how weak and useless Ember was, maybe he'd move on, then Ambrose could swoop in and pick him up. Then everything would be as it should be.

"Ambrose, I found the three plants!" Josie approached from the side.

"Shouldn't you be off boiling the roots?" This one needed a few extra brain cells. It would make things easier. *Maybe I should've cultivated Daisy. She seems smart enough and is a very loyal friend. Too late now.*

"The fire has gone out," Josie said, shrinking back.

Ambrose whipped around. "The fire in their camp never went out. When we checked on them, followed Daisy back, it was still lit. How did they do it? None of them even have fire magic!"

Cress came over and wrapped his arms around Ambrose's waist. She leaned into his heat and strength. He squeezed. "Exactly, love. They don't have your skills. They must've had one of the adults light it, someone who's been using fire magic for years. Just like for their cooler. They are completely relying on the adults to do everything for them. They're worthless, unlike us ... you."

She almost purred at his words. He had to be right. There was no other way Felix, Ember, and Daisy could have any hope of a fire. Felix was the only real power in that group, and he didn't use fire. Ambrose shifted her eyes to Josie. "Cress had a prank for today. I assume you have something planned for tomorrow?"

Josie's eyes lit up with mayhem. "Oh yeah. I can't wait!"

"Good. I want to make sure everyone knows that group failed this weekend's simple mission of finding plants in the woods. The three of them think they're better than us, and they must know they're nothing. Eventually, Ember will realize our school is no place for them and their human ways."

Josie's smile widened. "I assume we're hitting Simon and his brainiac group as well."

"Of course. Now stop trying to think. We need to get our part of the project done." Ambrose moved away before Cress's wandering hands reached their destination. She had to find a way to break up Ember and Felix and win him back. "Do we know anyone in Ember's air magic class? And what is Ember's third magical proficiency? Josie's questions this week have really gotten me thinking. What magic does Ember have? The only class you two have with them is earth magic, and that definitely isn't their forte."

Josie shrugged. "Once we're back at school, I'll ask around."

Ambrose knew what Josie meant by asking around and almost felt bad for anyone who stood between Josie and the information she was looking for.

She turned to Cress. "We should practice what we're going to say at next week's rally. While Josie sets up the next set of pranks, let's figure out what we'll say. We were good this week, but not great. I want to be the queen and king of the school."

Cress's smile was almost reptilian. "Yes, I agree. Everyone needs to know we're the ones who tell them what's what."

With a sway to her hips, Ambrose led the others back to camp. Once she got the fire going, she and Cress discussed how they'd entice more of the students to her father's and Tad Shade's movement.

Chapter 15 - Tit for Tat

Ember

Saturday morning came too early. Sitting up, Ember saw Daisy still sleeping next to them. The heat of the day threatened to bake them in their tent. They folded the sweatshirt over the pajama pants they'd slept in. The hole in the arm saddened them; they liked the sweatshirt. Why did the popular trio target them so much?

There was no reason! They sighed and got dressed. Jeans, a T-shirt, and shoes, and they were ready for the day.

Crawling out of the tent, Ember saw they were the first up this morning. They coaxed the fire back to life and began cooking oatmeal. Ember searched through everyone's bags and found dried fruit, nuts, and some brown sugar. Once the hot cereal was done, they scooped it into three bowls and began compiling what they wanted. A second pot of water began boiling, and they poured the water into a French press. The three had decided coffee was a necessity.

Ember had barely taken a bite when first Felix and then Daisy joined them. They ate in silence, none of them truly awake before they'd caffeinated.

As they finished their breakfast, Mr. Elias sauntered into their campsite. He wore jeans and a short-sleeved button-down shirt. His outfit was much more casual than his normal attire. He sat down on one of the logs, relaxed. It was nice having him come to check on them instead of a random parent. "Was your site set up like this with the logs when you got here?"

Daisy smirked. "With two air witches, moving some logs was a breeze, sir."

Both Ember and Felix groaned.

Mr. Elias looked at Ember. "Air magic? With the amount of razzing you let the others give you, if you can move one of these fallen trees, I'm surprised you don't stand up for yourself."

Felix tilted his head. "You didn't know?"

"What magic Ember can do? No. We aren't given that information. We just know that if you're students in our classes, you have something."

Ember shrugged. "I don't really feel like I have to prove anything to that group. Just because someone has a flashy magical ability or doesn't, there is no justification for bullying. I don't feel the need to show off to prove I have magic. I have always had friends and people I respected who didn't have magic, and doing things just to prove I was more seems ridiculous. I'm in your class to learn, not use my abilities."

The teacher made an approving sound. "Not a common teenager attitude, but one I can get behind."

"Is there a reason you're sitting with us? Hoping for some coffee?" Ember held up the French press with a bit of coffee left.

Mr. Elias's eyebrows rose. "I wouldn't say no to that. I came to check on how you secured your plants last night."

Daisy leapt up to get the plants while Ember poured a mug of coffee. Mr. Elias sighed as he took a sip. "I have some instant brown sludge I brought. Next year I'm bringing one of these. Coffee has risen on my priority list."

Once they'd gotten everything checked off and their teacher left, Ember ambled over to a stream a few minutes walk from the camp and rinsed everything off. They filled two buckets and added soap to one. They washed the dishes, dumping the water in some dirt, then slowly walked back to camp, their right ankle still tender.

The three of them were finally ready to head out to collect plants. They moved slower because of Ember's ankle, but they still moved. They had a dozen plants on the list, but they weren't expected to collect every one. This list contained plants that would be a great addition to what the school had in its stores but weren't that hard to find.

Within minutes, Ember spotted one of the plants they needed. Feeling good , they grabbed the shovel and dug out the plant, storing it in a plastic bag.

Ember decided to lead since their ankle was sore and they slowed down everyone's pace. Walking as quickly as they could, they searched the trees while Felix checked bushes and Daisy watched the ground for plants.

"Oh, there. That tree is flowering!" Ember started to move faster when their feet got caught in something and they ended up on their face in the mud. *In mud? Why is there mud? It hasn't rained in weeks.*

Ember searched the area. They lay in a wet, muddy patch. They pushed up and got to their knees. Behind them, stretched between two trees, was a thin wire. They went to rub their face but realized their hands were covered in the sticky goo. They wiped their hands on their shirt, but that just moved the filth around.

Daisy and Felix came up on either side of Ember, helping them to their feet. Felix spoke quietly as he used the bottom of his shirt to wipe their face. "Are you okay? How's your ankle?"

"I'm fine. Just a mess. If I can get the mud off my hands, I'll be fine." Ember grumbled low, wanting a warm bath, knowing one wasn't coming any time soon. Once on their feet, they pointed up at the flowering tree. "We can at least get the damn flower."

Daisy grunted. "I can't believe you're still thinking about class and the stupid list."

"What else? It isn't like we're going to fight back. It isn't worth it."

Daisy swung around. "Why not? You act like we have nothing. You have hidden talents. Felix is better than Cress in mind magic, not to mention thaumaturgy and earth magic. And I'm pretty darn good at earth, air, and water magic. We have skills. We just need to use them."

"Thaumaturgy magic only works if we know where they are. A small scale to big scale attack can't be blindly sent out. You know that," Ember said quietly, rubbing their hands on the nearest tree.

Daisy harrumphed. "What about mind magic?"

Felix sighed. "After Cress's attack, I put up protections on both your minds. They won't work long term, but they should hold for the rest of the weekend. I'm sure he's done the same for Ambrose and Josie. I could probably break down whatever he's done, but that would be it for me. It would knock me out. Breaking his hold on Ember last night wore me down."

Ember glared at the mud on the ground. "This pit was Josie's doing. She has earth and water proficiency. If she'd added ice right in front of it, she could've had her full trifecta going, but it's too warm for that. I wonder if Ambrose will try something with fire. I kind of hope she does. That would actually amuse me."

Ambrose may think she's the queen of the school and all powerful, but if she throws fire at me, she'll learn she's not the best at all things. I may have to put her in time-out.

Both Ember's friends gaped at them. Daisy spoke first. "You really think your skills, the ones you don't train at school, are up to defensive capabilities? And you'd let her find out?"

Ember shrugged and spoke low. They didn't know if anyone was nearby listening. "I'm not afraid of fire. And if you two are close to me, you don't have to worry either." Their trembling had stopped. "Look, I don't want others to know I can counter fire magic, but I'm not going to let Ambrose get away with anything either. There's a limit to my secrecy. I think my parents would agree. Safety first."

The three headed over to the flowering tree. With a bit of manipulation of air currents and air pressure, they got the branch low enough to collect some specimens.

After an hour of searching and collecting, they ran into the trio of bullies. Josie laughed hard enough that she needed to lean against a tree for support. "Wow, Ember, you look amazing. Great look. Is this the human version of roughing it chic?"

Ambrose's face remained neutral as she slowly shook her head. "Can't you even pretend to care about how you look?" She turned to Felix. "I don't know what you see in this one. They're a disgrace in every way." Back to Ember, one of Ambrose's eyebrows rose. "You know there's a stream nearby. You could clean yourself off, though that red hair of yours isn't going anywhere, is it? Such a shame. If it were a better color, you could be pretty."

Cress guffawed. "I don't agree. There's really no hope with this one."

As if a signal had been given, they turned and sauntered away. Josie flicked her arm up as if waving goodbye, and the ground beneath Ember rolled. If Felix hadn't caught them, they'd have fallen on their butt.

Ember watched them saunter away, anger burning through them. *What have I ever done to them? Why do they feel they have to pick on me? I keep to myself! I'm a nice person.* In a fury, Ember flicked their wrist, and a strong breeze cut through the trees, causing branches to rain down on the trio, scratching and slapping them.

Ambrose whipped around. Ember looked back, blankly. As Ambrose's gaze whipped to Felix, Ember turned towards him as well and saw his brow furrowed. Then they watched as Ambrose glared at Daisy, who looked shocked, eyes wide, mouth dropped open. Her glare finally fell on Ember, who shrugged. "Is something wrong?"

"You?"

Ember lifted their hands, deepening their shrug. "There was a breeze, Ambrose. Are you paranoid?"

With a squawk, she flung herself around and stomped away, Cress and Josie following.

Once they were all out of sight, Felix turned to Ember. "Was that a natural breeze?"

Daisy answered. "No. It absolutely wasn't. And I didn't cause it. What it was, was brilliant!" She started to bounce as they headed in the opposite direction as the mean kids.

Chapter 16 - A Swim in the Lake

Ember

Felix and Daisy were going to head back to camp to make lunch. Ember decided they needed to wash the mud from ... everywhere.

Before he left, Felix gazed into their eyes, his brown eyes reflecting concern. "Are you sure? You'll be off alone, and the water is awfully cold."

Ember shrugged. "I think I'll be fine. I'll watch where I'm going. The three jerks headed back to camp, secure in their win. I'm sure they're done with their shenanigans for now."

He touched his head with theirs. "I love your optimism. I don't know if it's well placed, but okay. Hurry back."

Not wanting to take too much time, Ember skipped along the winding trail as quickly as they could. Though the lake was hidden from view, there must have been a river that fed it, because they could hear the sounds of the small waves. They picked up their speed, though what they followed was nothing more than a game trail.

A box of dirt the size of a step grew in front of them faster than they could react, and they fell hard. This time, Ember didn't fall in mud. They slammed down onto hard ground. "Oof!" They shook their arm. A sharp pain radiated up to their elbow.

I'm going to have to do something about these injuries if they keep piling up. A sprained ankle, and this may be a broken arm. Ember took a calming breath. *It'll heal. Just don't react. Don't give the jerks the satisfaction.*

Laughter from behind Ember alerted them to watchers. They closed their eyes, and they felt a push of fire aimed at them. *Idiots.* With a small counter spell, they put out Ambrose's fire. A counter spell that should last awhile. Their dad had taught them well. Then they rolled to their feet and stood.

Ember heard whispers behind them.

A low male voice, it had to be Cress. "Ambrose, weren't you going to do something? I did my part."

"I don't know what happened. I was going to light that ugly top on fire, something small, nothing that would leave a mark. They're already on the ground. I'm sure they'd roll, but, ugh." Ambrose made a grunting sound as if she were shaking her hands. "I don't know what's happened. My fire magic hasn't failed me since I first began back in second year."

With a satisfied smile, Ember started walking to the water, pleasure flowing through them at being able to thwart at least one of the trio. They heard the voices retreat as they moved away from Ember and the water. Apparently watching them bathe wasn't on the agenda.

Once at the river, Ember debated going into the water with their clothes on. They could dry the clothes afterwards, but there would be no way to explain that to their friends. That level of fire magic skill was beyond any teen and most adults. Fire burned. It didn't dry clothes. Better to wear the dirty clothes back to camp and change then. Decision made, they stripped and folded their clothes behind a bush. They quickly slipped into the water, warming it directly around them. They dove down, trying to dislodge the dried dirt from their long, wavy hair.

They spent a few extra minutes under the water. They could pull some air down below the surface, prolonging their time in the serenity of the calming water. Ember knew they'd have to face the reality of the woods soon, filled with all those people. Not to mention their stomach kept speaking, letting them know they hadn't eaten enough today. But maybe just another minute or two ...

The dark calm of the water infused them, and a peace filled their soul. The woods were filled with schoolmates, but for a few minutes, Ember could pretend they were home alone, in their room, away from the insanity of this field trip. No Ambrose, no Cress, no Josie, no running around with a twisted ankle. And now the possibility of a broken arm. The thought of being away brought them joy.

Finally deciding it was time, Ember came to the surface and swam to the shore to gather their clothes. They were gone. They searched. Nothing. From the distance, they heard the running feet and laughter as the trio of evil ran off. The scent of burning cloth clinched what they'd done.

Ember wanted to bang their head against a rock. They'd been a fool. Of course the three bullies would take the soiled clothes. Burning them was a low beyond expectation, but now they knew the extent the trio would go to in their pranks. Ember had few options at this point. They could walk back to the tent naked. The trio was probably waiting with a camera just for that. Calling wouldn't work. They were too far from camp.

My best option isn't great. Someone may question why I suddenly have clean clothes. Then again, since no one would believe I have a dead magic and it's really the only option I have, what choice do I have? I'm not walking through these woods naked! I'll have to do some really fast talking ....

They let the serenity of the trees, the songs of the birds, and the peace of their swim sink back into them and focused. This was a larger bit of magic than they'd done in a long time. They reached out to the tent and hoped that Daisy wasn't inside. Thinking about where they'd left everything they brought, Ember reached for the pajama pants and sweatshirt they'd slept in. With a calming breath and a push, they called the clothes to the riverbank with the spatial magic they'd inherited from their mom.

A wave of dizziness threatened to take Ember down. They dropped to their butt ... hard, as two items of clothing appeared on the ground in front of them. Thankfully, the popular brats hadn't taken the shoes or socks. They were lying further under a bush. Ember had probably surfaced before they could find and take the items.

Pulling the soft warm clothing on felt like a hug. Ember almost purred with how nice it felt. They pulled on their footwear and slowly made their way back to camp.

They thought they heard a sound as they walked but weren't sure. *Has Josie been waiting to ambush me if I'd walked by naked? Did I ruin it all by having clothes?*

As they ambled towards the fire, Daisy leapt up to help. "How is your ankle? Are you okay?" Her brows furrowed. "Where did you get that outfit? You were wearing jeans and a T-shirt, not pajamas!"

Ember smiled. "Felix brought them for me so I'd have something warm and dry to wear after my wash."

Daisy spun so fast Ember thought she'd fall over. "You did? When?"

Felix gazed at Ember, eyes narrowed. Ember stared back, eyes wide, hoping he'd get the message. *Play along. I'll explain later.*

He licked his lips before slowly nodding. "When you headed out to skip to the loo. I realized putting on muddy clothing wouldn't be the best option."

Daisy's eyes softened. Ember thought she looked like the heart-eyes emoji. "That's so sweet. You two are, like, the cutest couple ever."

"That we are." Felix continued to stare at Ember before he finally turned to Daisy. "Do we have more of the s'mores fixings in your bag?"

"Be right back." She leapt up and darted into the tent.

He walked over and wrapped his arms around Ember's waist. "So, I brought you these clothes, did I? That was awfully considerate of me."

Ember leaned in, resting their forehead against his. "The treacherous threesome came back and snatched mine while I was in the water. Not only did they steal my clothes, I'm pretty sure they burned them. I was under the water at the time and couldn't stop them."

His voice got very low. "Is this why you have all these questions about spatial magic?"

Ember bit her lip and nodded.

He let out a big breath of air. "I don't know if I should be amazed, impressed, or sit you down and ask a million questions. You have more secrets than any one other person I know. Do your parents know?"

"I don't keep any secrets from them. They're the ones who train me." *They're the ones I get my abilities from, idiot.* Ember wasn't quite ready to tell him that, though they thought that should be obvious.

Daisy came out. "Okay, I have the dessert stuff, but let's have food first." She snorted when she saw them hugging. "Enough of that. Break it up! Now, we have some burgers we can cook with all ... well, most of the fixings. When an adult comes by, we need to get the ice in the cooler replaced."

Ember and Felix gathered the ingredients and started cooking. After burgers, they got marshmallows out to roast.

Daisy tilted her head back, getting the sticky treat into her mouth, as Ember decided their first pillowy treat looked done. Making a sandwich of the crackers and chocolate, they looked at their friend. "Did you get any of that in your mouth?"

Their friend snorted. "It isn't that bad!" She looked down and laughed harder. "Gah! I should change. I'll have half the woods stuck to me if I don't."

Ember bit their lip. "If it's okay with the two of you, I'd like to go out again while it's still light. See if we can find some more plants. It's barely after noon."

Felix leaned into them. "Are you sure? You've had a pretty bad day so far."

"I'm sure. I don't want to sit around here pouting until we head out after dinner. I'm sure we could find something to do for the next few hours, but spending another hour walking around and then resting would settle my nerves more."

Daisy bounded up. "Sounds good to me. We can wash these dishes then do another round about."

A tension relaxed in Ember at the thought of not letting the terrible trio run them to ground.

Chapter 17 - Everything Exploded out of the Tent ... Like a Glitter Bomb

Ember

Ember, Felix, and Daisy headed out in the opposite direction from earlier. They hoped it meant they wouldn't run into Ambrose, Cress, and Josie.

Instead of each looking in a different area, all three searched the trees, bushes, and ground together. They walked slowly and looked for any traps or tricks as well as the assigned plants. They had headed in a different direction but weren't going to be dumb. Pranks were a big part of this field trip.

Felix pointed at a tree. "Look there. It looks like someone set up some balloons with something in them. I wonder who got hit with that prank."

Ember shivered. "What would be in the balloons?"

Daisy laughed. "Anything, really. Food, glitter, syrup. I mean, the list is endless. Since I don't see glitter all over the place, I'm guessing something less ... awful."

"Gah!" Chills went down Ember's spine. "Please tell me you're joking. Mud's one thing, but glitter? That really *is* evil."

Daisy found the first plant, wormwood. She grabbed the shovel and made quick work of shoveling it up. It went into a storage box in the shoulder bag. As she boxed the specimen, Felix saw a small shrub they wanted to collect leaves and stems from, rue.

Ember began to feel excitement boil as they got into a groove.

Once everything was secure, they headed further from camp. As they walked, they heard voices. Ember's gut clenched. Two female voices and a male voice. Nothing they wanted to deal with.

Slowly creeping around a corner, Ember saw Olivia, Tansy, and Simon. Olivia's hands were on her hips as she glared at Simon. "Yes, Simon, we understand that. You aren't the only one who knows these things. If you're going to continue to be so arrogant, just go away, and meet us later at camp."

He grumbled, "That isn't how this works, Olivia. We're supposed to work together."

Tansy rolled her eyes and saw Ember. "Then work with us and stop being a jerk. Hi, Ember, how are you all doing?"

"Good. Sounds like you all are having fun. Have you run into anyone else?"

Simon spun on his heel. Then his eyes narrowed as he spied Ember. "Are you wearing pajamas? Is this how you dress when you aren't in school? The more I get to know about you, the less impressed I am."

They snorted. *Right back atcha, buddy.* "I'm very worried about your opinion, Simon. I'll make sure to upgrade my wardrobe to meet your standards."

Tansy laughed. "You really should. I mean, will you be able to sleep at night if he isn't impressed with you?"

Ember smiled wide but stopped themself from laughing.

A red sheen took over Simon's face. "No, you're the first other students we've seen—why? Are you working with others? You know you aren't supposed to. The point is figuring this out yourself. Are you cheating?" His tone got a nasty bite at the last words.

"You need to back down, Simon," Daisy snapped, stepping forward. "Some teams are playing pranks, not cheating. You know this. You've been in the school district long enough to know the stories. Stop being mean."

Eyes wide, Simon's blush increased. "You're right. Yeah, sorry." He gazed at Ember again. "So a prank then ... was it a bad prank?"

Ember shook their head, tired of him. "Just mud, lots of mud."

Tansy smiled. "Thus the pajamas."

Felix slid his hand in theirs. "Anyway, Simon, you're correct. No working with others. We'll be off. Good luck, you three." Ember realized he'd taken Daisy's hand as well. He was showing Simon that they were a team and were working together. They smiled as they headed off.

The day was beautiful as they walked through the trees. There were a few birds chirping and a warm breeze. They found a few more ingredients, but eventually, Ember's ankle began to throb. "I think I'm done. Let's head back and relax."

Felix wrapped his arm around them. "On the bright side, I think I found some of the plants for tonight."

Daisy clasped their free hand. "I found some as well. We'll be in bed before midnight, one at the latest. We can actually sleep tonight."

Footsteps crunching through the underbrush caused the three of them to pause. Ember didn't want to see or talk to anyone else. They were tired of people. Having been homeschooled, this much time with other people was fraying their nerves.

Again, Ember wondered why their parents thought this was such a great idea. They had to give up a secret about their skill with fire, they may have given up a second, and they'd been picked on by crazy popular bullies. But, in the end, they did have some good memories with Daisy and Felix.

Bracing themselves, Ember waited to see who would walk around the bend. A moment later, an adult sauntered into view, another of the parent volunteers. "Oh, hi. I'm doing rounds today, checking in on campsites. Is everything okay? Do you need anything?"

Daisy stepped forward. "We could use more ice in our cooler."

He held out a map, and Daisy pointed to which campsite was theirs. He nodded. "I'll swing by there now and refresh your ice. My freeze should last twenty-four hours, so you should be good until tomorrow, unless you leave the box open." With that, he spun on his heel and left.

The three followed in the direction the man had gone. He walked faster than Ember wanted to on their hurt ankle. When they got back, they could feel the chill emanating from their cooler.

Ember pulled away from Felix and stretched. "I'm going to go lie down for a bit."

"Me too," Daisy agreed. "We didn't get much sleep last night, and tonight won't be much better. Even if we're just reading or lounging, some downtime sounds nice."

Felix headed to the fire pit as Ember followed Daisy to their tent. They kept their tent tightly zipped regardless of if they were in it or not so nothing got in. Neither of them wanted a surprise in their clothes. There may not have been anything poisonous in these woods, but that didn't mean things couldn't bite.

Inside the tent, they flopped on their bed. Looking up, Ember saw it.

Above them, on the ceiling of the tent, was an orange ... spider? It looked like a scorpion. The body was blackish in the center, but mostly orange. It was about three inches long. The head was oval shaped with a pointy-tipped end. *Is that a mouth?* It had eight orange legs ... *eight legs. Yep, that thing is a spider. A really big spider. A huge spider. How did something that big get into our tent? That can't have just wandered in. It's another prank. Those jerks put a monster of a spider in our tent.*

"Um ... Daisy?" Ember couldn't look away. The spider hadn't moved, but terror flowed through them. "We have ... ah ... um ... a visitor." Their voice went up at the end, almost like they asked a question.

Daisy squealed as if in delight, then out of the corner of their eye, Ember saw Daisy's head swing from the door of the tent to the top. "Oh my gods!" She bellowed. "A spider? Those jerks. I hate them!"

She made enough noise to wake the dead ... or to bring Felix in from the fire. Ember heard the zipper and then his calming voice. "Okay, it's just a camel spider. Big, scary-looking, but its bite is only deadly to shifters, specifically phoenixes. And to them, they always come back, so it isn't a final death. Again, final death for a phoenix—"

"Oh my gods, Felix, stop with your obsession." Daisy sounded exasperated. "We can't sleep with that thing in here."

"It probably won't do anything. Spiders like that just hang out. The likelihood of a bite is small."

Ember moaned in despair and watched, as if in slow motion, the orange beast dropped down from the tent's roof.

Daisy screamed.

From the corner of their eye, Ember saw Felix put a hand on Daisy's arm, trying to get her to relax. Felix's voice flowed in reassuring tones. "No one will get hurt. Once it lands, we'll catch it. On the off chance it does bite one of us, everyone will be okay."

Ember tried to say something, but they couldn't get sound beyond the sudden terror swamping their system.

A light pressure of the thing landing on their arm. They didn't move. Maybe it would scurry away. *Breathe ... try to breathe!*

Ember trembled with fear.

More screams, and Ember tensed.

A sharp pain as the spider bit Ember's arm. In a flash, Ember magically pushed all their belongings out of the tent. Bags crashed outside.

Dread like they'd never felt before engulfed them. They found their voice. "Both of you, get out of here, now! Take anything you can, but go, get away from me. Hurry!"

Silence.

"Go!"

Chapter 18 - A Memory

Ember

"Daddy, can I take a bike ride?"

"Oh, sweety, I'm very busy right now. I can't take you out, and Mom's at the store."

"But Daddy, I'm five! I can do it alone. I know how to be careful. You and Mommy have splained the rules to me before."

She watched her Daddy, hoping he'd let her go. It would be her first time biking by herself, and the thought made her wiggly.

Moving away from his desk, he knelt on the ground next to her. Daddy was really tall. Her dad wrapped his strong arms around her. "Will you be extra careful, Ember? You know how worried Mommy and I get."

She started to bounce. She knew this meant she could go. "Yes! Super-duper extra duper super careful."

He kissed both her cheeks and her forehead. "Okay, my sweetheart. Make sure you wear your helmet."

"I will, Daddy!" She was off before she'd finished the last word, her red hair flying into her eyes. She wiped at her face to clear her vision. The new helmet her parents got her would help with that. It was the only good thing about the silly hat. It kept her hair out of her face while she rode, no matter how windy it got.

They lived on a large block, but there was a street that didn't go all the way through. Mommy called it a cul-de-sac. Ember didn't like riding into that street with the circle at the end because there was a boy in one of the houses who teased her and chased her with a stick.

She rode out of the garage on her purple bike, and excitement surged through her. She was finally riding her bike alone. She was a big girl now! When she got to the corner, she debated riding along the sidewalk. Crossing the street was dangerous, and there was a car waiting to turn into the very busy street.

She bit her lip and debated turning around. Riding back and forth in front of her house would be a lot of fun too. Just being outside on her bike without any adults was pretty amazing.

Just then she saw the driver of the car, a blonde woman with a nice face, who waved at her, telling her to go. The woman had a nice smile and nodded as if to say riding across the street would be swell. *Daddy likes saying swell. It was a funny word.*

Ember waved back and started across the street. *A woman waving me across the street and watching me is almost the same as having my parents with me, right?*

To her left, the traffic zoomed by. The street was very busy with lots of cars that liked to drive very fast. Many of them used their horns to yell at each other. Ember wished she could bike as fast as those cars. It would be cool. Her hair would fly back in the wind. But no, on her bike, she barely went faster than her daddy walking with his long legs.

She heard the car next to her, the one with the nice lady, rev its engine, then she went weightless. For a moment, Ember thought about how it felt like flying and how much she liked to fly, but then she realized, as she was, flying wasn't right. The next thing she knew, there was a crashing sound. Pain, fire, and everything went black.

"Did the boy survive?"

"I'm here on the scene. It's been just over an hour, and the ambulance rushed the boy to the local hospital. Reports say he was biking across the street and hadn't checked for cross traffic. The woman who hit the boy is traumatized."

"I would imagine. That boy landed in the middle of busy traffic. Any word on the fire?"

"There's an ongoing investigation, but it looks like the boy hit a car that ran into a truck. Somehow, the car hit the truck at just the right angle to ignite the truck's gas tank. Despite being in this horrific accident, authorities believe the boy will survive. So far, no one else seems to have been hurt."

"That's amazing."

"It really is. Well, I'll let you know if we learn anything else. For now, this is Dan Jansen, reporting live—" The TV stopped making noise, and Ember groaned. There wasn't any pain, but the sudden stillness in the room made her dizzy and confused.

A cool hand touched her forehead. "Ember, dear, are you awake?"

"Mommy, why do I feel so weird? What happened?"

Mommy's voice was soft, and her hand stroked down Ember's face to her cheek. "I was hoping you could tell us."

"The lady in the car waved me to cross. Then her engine made a noise, then there was more noise and fire, and I'm here. Can we go home?"

She heard a scraping sound and footsteps. Her daddy's voice. "We're going to take our child home."

"We want to run a few more tests on your son."

"He's fine. I'll sign any waivers you need signed. He's awake; he's talking—I'm going to take him home."

Mommy gave her, wait, no, *him,* clothes. They'd warned him about this. "Go change in the bathroom, hon."

It was the first time Ember's body had changed. Daddy's body had changed once. Ember used to have two moms. She'd ... Ember sighed, he'd have to learn a few new things. Everything seemed different ... all because that woman waved her ... no him ... no them on. It would be easier to use something neutral.

Chapter 19 - Secrets Learned, Secrets Created

Felix

The tent was on fire. Everything was burning.

The only reason everything would burn, and Ember would kick their friends out, and they were so good with fire, and a spider would scare them ...

Felix couldn't believe the only conclusion he could come to, but there was only one ... *Ember is a phoenix.*

Ember is a phoenix*?!*

Oh my gods ... Ember is a phoenix.

"Ember is in there. The tent is burning. What do we do? Felix, what's going on?" As Daisy spoke, her voice got more and more frantic. "We have to get Ember out!"

Ember is a phoenix, and Daisy is freaking out. Breathe, focus, and think. What do I do? Ember wouldn't want anyone else knowing. I have to help Ember keep their secret. They've obviously kept it ... forever. I have to help them, but can I? Is this enough justification?

"Daisy, fill the wash buckets with water before this spreads. I'll save Ember. Don't worry."

"Okay." Her eyes were as large as saucers, and her head jerked up and down.

She ran off.

Felix knew the fire had to be put out. Smoke was billowing up, but not much more than a campfire. He wanted to give Ember time. He didn't know how much time they needed but knew they needed some amount of time. Soon, Daisy would remember she could just pull water up with her magic, and then he'd have to figure out a new plan.

He moved to the remaining bits of tent, covered in fire. Finding a long stick, he flipped the burning parts away. All he found was a pile of ash.

As he gazed, his breathing almost stopped. Phoenix ash. It was really true. This wasn't a weird prank.

Daisy ran up and dumped the water on the burning tent. She spun and took two steps before she stopped and slowly turned back. "Where is Ember?" Her head jerked around looking for her friend. All the color drained from her face when she didn't see them.

Felix gazed at Daisy and then at the ash that started to stir. "Ember is safe. Don't worry." He wasn't sure how long this would take, but he knew that this was a secret Ember wanted to keep ... had to keep. It was about safety as much as protection.

Can I do this? Can I not do it? Do I have a choice?

He pulled Daisy to the fire and sat her down with her back to the tent. "Give me a second, then we'll get that fire out."

Daisy looked confused but trusted him. "Okay, but quick. I need to get more water." She waved the buckets.

He placed his hand on the back of her neck. He loved doing mind magic. It felt natural to him, but not when it meant messing with memories. Beyond the idea of messing with something that defined a person, it was illegal.

But this is the safety of a family of phoenixes. If Ember is a firebird, then so is one of their parents? Both of them? Gods above, they've been hiding in plain sight. But then again, this is Daisy, a friend. What right do I have to mess with her memories?

Doubt and confusion warred in him.

"Felix, what are we doing here?" The urgency in Daisy's voice broke through his resolve.

"Okay. I'm sorry. I'm really, really sorry." Since he was a juvenile, if he was caught, he'd get a single warning. Adults had their magic bound. But this was bigger than him.

He closed his eyes and held his hands out. Daisy, full of trust in their friendship, placed her hands on his. Her trust nearly ripped his heart out. He found the memories surrounding the spider, the bite, and the fire.

Ember feared the spider. After it bit them, in a knee-jerk reaction, they spit out a bit of fire that got out of control and burned down the tent. They survived and are fine.

He quickly looked over his shoulder at the ashes that swirled. The cloud was too thick to see through. *Please be okay.*

Once the new memories were set, Daisy slumped. Memory shifts always left the target in a light slumber for a few minutes. Daisy would probably sleep for ten to fifteen minutes. Hopefully that would be enough time for Ember. He had no idea. In all his research on phoenixes, this never came up.

He found a blanket and covered Daisy then ran to the river himself to get another bucket of water. He'd never wished for a water proficiency before.

He quickly put out the flames on each of the bits of tent material. He didn't want the flames to spread or attract the attention of anyone else in the woods. Then he checked over the stored plants. Ember had thrown the bags from the tent, and it appeared like they'd survived. He stacked everything outside his tent.

Checking out the congealing ash, he realized Ember's body was formed, but it was different. It would appear there were a lot of things that the phoenixes had kept secret.

Chapter 20 - The Package Has Changed, but the Person Is the Same

Ember

Ember woke up to the swirling ash of death around them. They pounded their fists on the ground but bit back the scream. They wanted to yell. Images flashed through their mind. Mud pit, river, plants, orange spider ... that was it. The stupid spider. *"It isn't poisonous unless you're a dumb phoenix."*

With a grunt, Ember pulled themself to sitting. They sat in the tattered remains of the tent, a soggy puddle of the bottom of the tent but no sides. It had all burned down. *Because of me and my fire. How much of the campsite was destroyed?*

Pulling their knees up, they rubbed their forehead. This wasn't happening. The biggest family secret was the fact that they and their father were phoenixes, and here they were, dead and back again.

Who knew? Felix? Daisy? Did anyone else see the fire and their reemergence? Did the whole school know? The whole town? Did one prank by the biggest jerks in school out their family to the world? With a groan at the enormity of what just happened, everything sank in. "No no no." They groaned. "This can't be real."

Felix's voice reached them from the direction of the firepit. "Ember, are you okay?"

They slowly lifted their gaze and met his warm brown eyes, deep with concern. Ember pulled their legs in tighter. *What would Felix think?* A tear threatened to burn a trail down their cheek.

"Can you find me something to wear?"

"Yeah, of course."

Ember heard a zipper and the sounds of movement. "Here, I grabbed one of my sweatshirts. It's a bit bigger than yours, it will ... it should cover things better. I have my sweatpants too. If that's okay?"

It only took a moment to slip into the soft, warm clothes. As they dressed, they took in their 'new' body. It had been a few years since they'd had these parts, but they were pretty sure they knew how everything worked. They weren't sure if they preferred female or male bits better, but they knew they didn't want to move. They liked the school, despite the mean crowd, and their friends. That said, they knew what their parents would say. The pattern had been the same their whole life.

Felix's clothes fit well. They were soft and made Ember feel like he was hugging them. With a sigh, they said to Felix's back, "Thanks."

Ember took a moment to check out the surroundings. Though the tent was a soggy mess, it looked like Felix and Daisy had saved just about everything else. Ember didn't see any other spectators, so maybe there was a chance to mostly save the family secret after all.

Felix slowly turned back to face them. "Can you ... how do you feel? Are you okay to walk? To move around?" He finally gazed at them.

Ember snorted and tried to hide their trembling hands by pacing the length of the campsite. They appreciated that Felix seemed to be ignoring the elephant in the room, or rather, the shifted body in the woods. "Oh, I'm great. After that, all my injuries are healed. Best care medicine can buy, all it costs is my ... gods, sorry. I don't mean to be nasty. I just ..." They didn't know what to say.

"You're just trying to process everything. Your secret was just revealed ... or rather, secrets. There seem to be several. And I'm sure whatever just happened to you was ... weird. I get it. You also don't need to worry. I'm not going to tell anyone."

"What about Daisy? Where is she? I love her as a best friend, but she isn't the best with the big secrets." Ember looked around again but didn't see her.

"I took care of that. She thinks you used a bit of fire magic to kill the spider. Too bad the tent is dust ... unless. There were extras in the bottom of the bus. Any chance ..." He looked at Ember hopefully then off towards where the buses were.

They took a deep breath. After an ordeal, Ember usually avoided anything big, but keeping their secret was important. They bit their lip and closed their eyes. Searching with their mind, they found the buses and where the extra tents had been stored. They were so heavy and the distance so damn far!

This is to keep your secret. If the tent is fixed, others won't ask questions. Even if you black out ... it's worth it.

Digging deep into their magical reserve, something they didn't have much of only being half-witch, Ember gave it their all. They pushed more magic into their spatial pull than they'd ever done, then, head spinning, slumped. Ember would've fallen over if Felix hadn't caught them.

"That was brilliant. Can you help me put it up?"

"I need a few minutes. I'm dizzy."

"Okay, let me get this cleaned up."

Daisy came over, wobbling on her feet. "Oh, you got us a tent to replace what we had. Good job. Let me clear the dust." She waved her hands, and a gust of wind blew all the debris away. She and Felix quickly got the new tent up. Afterwards, she came and sat next to Ember. "You know, you should talk to your parents about that fire magic. I know it's a secret and all, but using it to kill a spider only really killed our tent. You need more control, my friend." She laughed.

Eyes wide, Ember opened their mouth to respond.

Daisy held up a hand. "I know. That's it. I won't mention fire magic again. I'm done. You don't have it, as far as I know. Now that we have a replacement and everything is back to normal, it's all good."

Ember's mind whirled at the power of mind magic. They really needed to figure out if there were any protections against it.

Daisy shot up. "Okay, I'm going to bring our stuff into the tent and get it all fixed up. Then we can all get some sleep." And off she went.

Felix came over and wrapped an arm around Ember. "You doing okay?"

"I don't know. You saw what happens to a phoenix when they resurrect. It's a secret that isn't really known."

His arm tightened on their waist. "And?"

"And? And I'm no longer the person you were dating, Felix. Who I am, what I feel, it's all the same. Just the outside has changed. Throughout my life, my family has moved every time I've resurrected, just in case. I don't want to move, despite everything. I like the school. I like my friends. I really like you. But ..." Ember didn't know how to ask what Felix's feelings were to having the person he dated change from having typical female parts to typical male parts.

Felix's warm hands moved up to Ember's face, and he pulled them in for a quick kiss. "It's you I love. You are still you. You are still beautiful. I know that you don't want others to know what happened ... you're going to have to figure that out. But to me, I don't really care what's under all this. It's the person I've fallen for, okay? You could come to school looking however you wanted, and I'd be happy to tell everyone that we are dating. So, if it's me you're worried about, don't be." Then he winked. "And in my clothes, you almost look the same. Daisy didn't even notice."

It felt like a weight had been lifted. In all Ember's life, they never thought they'd find anything like what their parents had. Someone who accepted them for who they were.

Chapter 21 - Finishing the Assignment

Ember

A nap did wonders for Ember's mood. Their rebirth had healed them. Their ankle no longer hurt, and their arm felt fine. In their current body, they were a bit stronger, though they probably should hide that from Daisy. The next big hurdle was going home and explaining everything that had happened to their parents. They hadn't lied when they said they predicted their family would move, but they really didn't want to leave the community they'd created. *Would there be any way to convince Mom and Dad that sticking around would be the best decision?*

Ember, Felix, and Daisy met around the fire and made sandwiches. They had lunch meat, cheese, and bread. It was quick and easy. There was about an hour before the moon fully rose and they could head out for their final round of plant-gathering.

Daisy's pep was just as high as it always was. "Okay, when we were out earlier, I saw a few of the night plants. Felix, you said you did as well. I know your ankle isn't well, Ember. Do you want to hang back here or head out with us?"

Ember bit their lip. *If I hang back I could go pull my own prank on the terrible trios campsite ... but no, that isn't what we're doing.* "My ankle feels a lot better. It was only a twist. They never seem to stay painful long. I'll happily head out with you two."

"Excellent. I'd hoped you would say that. The dream team is at it again." She reached into the cooler. "Drinks?" She handed out a soda to each of them.

"I'll have a soda, if you're offering." Cress's voice came from behind them. "I'm sure Ambrose and Josie wouldn't mind one as well."

With a sigh, Ember cracked open their soda and turned. The evil trio of doom stood on the edge of their camp. "What are you three doing in our camp?"

Cress chuckled. "We just wanted to make sure everything was okay here. We were worried you may be hurt or upset."

Daisy shrugged. "Why? Is there something wrong with our camp that we should be worried about?"

Cress's face hardened. "No, of course not. We saw smoke before and got curious."

Ember made a dramatic pantomime of looking around their camp and shrugging.

Felix's head tilted. "When did you see smoke, and what made you think it was our camp?"

Ambrose rolled her eyes. "Like a few hours ago, and because we have the map, we can read who's camp is in this direction."

"It's not the only camp, and if you were so worried, why wait so many hours? If your concern were real, you would've shown up ages ago. Obviously, you thought we'd left already. I think you should leave. You can see we're finishing our meal, and you're ruining it. We all have an assignment to do, though I'm guessing you have people to do yours. Have you done any of your own work, Ambrose, or have you just duped Josie or other adults into doing all the work for you?" Felix stared at her until, with a small huff, Ambrose turned and left.

Once they were out of sight, Daisy grumbled, "Dumb popular idiots. I bet they were hoping we were cowering about the dumb spider. They came to see their handiwork. How can they be so bad at school but understand so much about the movement?"

Ember bit back a response and saw Felix's face harden.

"They probably *were* coming to check on that damn spider," Ember agreed. "Let's just get our last batch of moon light ingredients and call this field trip a win ... or at least, not a complete loss? Do you think our stuff is safe?"

Felix nodded. "They need to gather plants, and this is when the majority of teachers and volunteers are out monitoring our movements."

Daisy scoffed, then smiled wide. "What are you talking about? It's been amazing! This has been everything I hoped it would be. Hanging out with you two has been perfect." She kissed her fingers in a chef's kiss.

Ember wasn't sure what trip Daisy had been on, but they were glad someone had enjoyed the school event.

Having found the plants in advance, heading out and picking them took little time. Felix led them to the two he knew about. Ember harvested one, Felix the other. Then Daisy darted to the next plant. They were back to camp so early, Ember couldn't believe that the whole trip could've been that easy. For some groups it may have been.

Once everything was stored and ready for transport back to the buses and then school, Daisy grabbed the sandwich cookies and frosting. They made sandwiches with the frosting center. Ember thought they'd vibrate through the log they sat on with sugar overload. That didn't stop them from having seconds and thirds. They *were* teens after all.

Once they'd had a few delectable desserts, Daisy yawned. "I'm crashing. I'll see you two in the morning."

Felix clasped Ember's hand. "Would you mind staying up a bit longer?"

They shrugged, though a boulder landed in their gut. *This won't be good.*

Listening to the tent zipper close, Felix pulled a few sodas from the bag and handed one to Ember. "Can you tell me about ... well, you? Daisy isn't wrong about my obsession, and I figure this is as private as we'll get. That, and, I'd love to actually get to finally know about you. We've been dating for two years, and I'd like a chance to finally meet you."

Ember bit their lower lip. They weren't sure if this would be a good idea, but at this point, Felix knew they were a phoenix, and there was no going back. "Well, I'll tell you this. Phoenixes are accident-prone. If there is a chance for something bad to happen to them, it will. Once I saw the spider, I knew there was no way for me to get out of that trap alive."

"Really?"

"Yeah. It's kind of weird, but true. We're highly unlucky. It's one reason I avoid confrontation so much. It doesn't take much for me to end up as a pile of ash."

"And every time you reincarnate, you shift sexes?"

They smiled. "Yeah, it's super weird."

"I don't know. It's kind of cool too." He squeezed their hand. "But I may be partial because it's you. Do you tend to feel better one way or another? You don't have to answer that if you don't want to. It's just so interesting."

Ember leaned into him and shut their eyes. They spoke low so no one could overhear, but they lowered their voice more. They didn't want to take any chances. "I was born and assigned female at birth. My first change was at five. I kind of knew what was happening, but not really. I had to relearn a lot of things. I've had this body before, but, yeah, I think I prefer the other one. But that may be because I've had it for the last three years. Give me a couple weeks, and I may change my mind. You know, familiarity breeds comfort."

He laughed. "That makes sense. Do you think you'll let people at school know, then?"

Ember froze. "No, I don't think so. That would take more explaining than I'm ready to give. I think for now I'll stick with baggy clothing. I just hope I can convince everyone I'm still the same person under these clothes."

"Good thing the weather's getting colder." He winked. "Or, you know, you could always off yourself again."

They groaned. "As fun as that could be, it still hurts." Ember almost laughed at the understatement. "I'd rather avoid it."

"How will your parents react?"

Ember sighed. "That's the big question, isn't it?"

Chapter 22 - The Decision

Ember

The next morning was a whirlwind of action. The three of them brought down the tents while snacking on trail mix, marshmallows, and sandwich cookies. Ember had woken early, nervous about what they'd tell their parents, so they had coffee to drink as well.

Once everything was stored, including the plants they'd so carefully prepared, they suited up with all their belongings attached to their bodies. All three of them did one more visual check. Secure in the knowledge that they had everything they'd brought in, they followed the path they'd taken into the woods back out.

When they got to the bus, they stuffed all their bags into the bottom storage area and climbed in. Daisy clutched her pillow and leaned it on the window for the five-minute ride back to the school, closing her eyes as if she could sleep in that time. Once there, Ember climbed out, said their goodbyes, and began their walk home. Most people had rides. Felix offered them one, but Ember wanted the time to decompress before seeing their parents and, more importantly, having their parents see them.

I really don't want to move again. As hard as it is with some of the kids at the school, it's better than starting over. I have to figure out a way to convince them staying is better.

Once in the house, they dashed up the stairs to drop off their stuff. They emptied their bag, putting their clothes and toiletries away. Felix had taken all of the plants for class, and Daisy had gathered the food. Ember only had their own personal effects.

As they put the last of their clothes in their hamper, the door opened, and their mom walked in. "Hey, hon, how did it—" she stopped for a moment, and Ember saw her face tighten with dread. "Oh, oh no. Ash! Come quick!"

Ember heard their dad running. Once both their parents were in the room, Ember sat on the edge of the bed with their mom. Dad took the desk chair.

"What happened? Tell us everything."

It took a while, but they tried to detail all of the events of the outing. They finished with, "I think this was why I didn't want to go. The other kids at school aren't very nice. Well, most of them are, but there are a few, and I figured they wouldn't be nice during an unsupervised couple of days in the woods. I'm not sure why those three have targeted me, but they have."

Dad looked ready to explode. "I can't believe the antics the school gave a blind eye to. They allowed all of that to go down? It's negligent."

Mom sighed. "To most, that spider, though terrifying, isn't deadly. It would've left a welt on my arm but nothing more."

"But what about the rest? Tripping Ember? The mud, burning their clothes?" Dad sat taller, his arms waving to emphasize his points. "It's all abuse and humiliation. We need to go to the school and complain. No, we should leave. Look at Ember. You shifted. This can't get out. We've spent too much time protecting ourselves. Who knows?"

Ember wrung their hands together. "Only Felix. He knows this is a big secret and changed Daisy's memories so she doesn't know." Ember filled their parents in on the rest of the story.

Their mom sighed. "So Felix fixed Daisy's memory so she doesn't remember what you are, but Felix knows. That's both good and bad. I trust him in theory, but he's just a kid. How can he be expected to keep a secret this big? It was hard enough for you to keep it all these years. This could be life or death. It's believed that phoenixes are extinct. For the school, the city, the world, to know that two are alive, I don't know. It scares me."

Ember felt the weight of it all land squarely on their shoulders. "It scares me too, Mom."

Dad's face hardened. "It's time to start packing. We can't stay here. As much as I want to make a big deal at the school. Maybe I could make a big deal and use that as the reason I'm pulling Ember from that hellhole. How dare they endanger our kid!"

It felt like a punch to their gut. "Please. I don't want to go back to homeschooling. I really like it here. I like my friends. Why can't I just wear baggy clothes? I can pull off not having changed. I can dress the part. No one will have to know."

"I don't know that you can, hon." Mom looked sad. "It is a big request."

"I want to stay. Doesn't that matter at all?" They tried not to sound pitiful. They wanted to come up with a strong argument, but they felt their world crumbling around them.

A sadness filled the room. Dad started to speak, but Mom shook her head. "I know you want to stay. You wanted to stay in the last house as well, but, hon, we're really talking about safety for all of us. In the end, that has to be the thing we focus on the most."

Ember slumped. They knew that they weren't going to win the fight. In the end, the family would move. They'd moved every time they'd died and resurrected. This wouldn't be any different. It was always about safety first.

They looked around their room with the bed and dresser, small desk and nice-sized closet. They were all things. They'd leave the things and just take the small items, anything that fit in a small moving van. When they landed in the next location, they'd get new things.

Ember's parents had a few lifelong friends they trusted to come in behind them and sell the house and the contents of their home. They'd eventually get the money, but the family had enough. Dad was old, really old. Maybe the oldest being in the world. He'd been investing money his whole life, and because of that, they were rich. From the outside, someone may not have been able to tell, but it was true. Despite everything Ambrose said, Ember's family probably had more power and money than hers.

As for Mom's age, a magic user, Ember wasn't sure. Some of her stories seemed to go back to the War of Peace, but magic users had the same lifespan as regular humans. When Ember asked, their mom always said they'd talk about that later, at another time.

"Let's have pizza for dinner. How does that sound?"

Ember gazed at Mom, numb. They didn't care what they had. They were frustrated about having to pack. "Sure, sounds great."

They got up and headed to the kitchen. Dad got on his phone and started putting in their order.

Ember selected a soda and sat at the table, defeated. "How long until we leave? Can I have a few more days at school? Say goodbye to my friends?"

Their mom's face drooped. "I don't really think that's a good idea. If you say goodbye, they'll want to know why you're leaving. You'll have to have a reason. That will lead to more questions. In my experience, it's best if we just ... disappear. We have people who will create a cover story for where we went."

"So, I'm just done? No more Feniks Secondary School? No more Ambrose, Cress, and Josie bullying me? Not that that part's bad. No more Daisy, my best friend who's almost like a sister?" Ember sniffled, trying to fight back tears. "No more Felix?" Though the idea of the bullying ending sounded nice, the last two hurt. They wanted to cry. Their body trembled as they sat there, emotions roiling in them.

"I'm sorry, but that is the safest way. I know this was your first school, the first time you had access to this many people your age. A chance for you to socialize with people your own age and not just be around your dad and me." Her face softened, and she reached out to squeeze Ember's hand. "Your first boyfriend. But in the end, this is the way it has to be. I think we'll plan on leaving in a couple of days. We'll spend the time packing. Tomorrow, Dad will get a truck, and we can spend the time filling it."

"But you don't get it. Felix, he—"

The doorbell rang. *Finally, food. Maybe that will fill the hole building in my life.*

Standing, Ember went to get the pizza order. They realized their parents wouldn't care what Felix thought of them and their new body. That wouldn't sway them one way or another in their decision to uproot Ember.

Trying to hold onto their dignity, Ember wiped their eyes and took a steadying breath. The last thing they needed was the pizza delivery guy gawking at them for crying as they grabbed the order.

Finally feeling presentable, Ember opened the door.

Standing on the stoop was Felix and his parents.

Chapter 23 - Telling Tales

Ember

"Mom, Dad, um, it isn't the pizza."

Dad made it to the door first. "Oh, Mr. and Mrs. Porter, it's a ... good to see you. We weren't expecting you."

Dad just stood there, a blank look on his face, not letting them in or shutting the door in their faces. As if he were a statue, he just stared at the trio on the stoop. The tension grew more and more awkward.

Felix's dad nodded. "It's good to see you too, Mr. Savita. Could we please come in? There's something we'd like to speak to you about."

It took a few seconds before Dad finally stepped back, shook his head, and waved his arm. "Yeah, fine."

Apprehension filled Ember as they walked to the kitchen table. They shot Felix a look, but he was leading his parents to the table.

Mom asked if they wanted wine or soda then brought out a bottle of red wine for the adults. She selected a few cans of soda and glasses on her second trip, placing everything on the table. Felix, sitting next to Ember, handed them a soda and took one himself. Dad poured the adults wine.

The doorbell rang again, and this time, Mom went to answer it. It was the pizza. Mom came back with four boxes that she put on the counter.

Dad smiled. "I thought we'd have left overs for tomorrow, but I guess we have enough for everyone."

Mrs. Porter smiled. "Mr. Savita, you don't have to feed us, you know."

Dad's smile turned into a scowl. "As long as you're in our house and we have food, it's fine. Eat. It's a small thing. And please, it's Ash, and she's Sadie. All these Mr. and Mrs. will drive me batty."

Mrs. Porter relaxed. "Sounds good. Call me Bonny." She patted her husband's chest with the back of her hand. "Conner."

Mom handed out plates, and everyone filled them before sitting back down.

Mr. Porter took a sip of the wine then placed his glass down. "Our son spoke to us about what happened in the woods."

Ember's head fell into their hands, and they groaned. Just when they thought things couldn't get worse. *He promised not to tell anyone!* Their parents' nightmare coming true. Their biggest secret getting out.

Felix quickly said, "Just what Daisy knows. I thought I'd let you tell the rest."

Mom and Dad both visibly relaxed at his words.

Before either Mom or Dad could say anything, Mr. Porter continued. "Please don't be upset with Felix. From what I understand, you are as open with Ember as we are with Felix. We have no ... or very few secrets," he amended when he took in everyone's reaction to Felix's words. "Felix mentioned the weekend's events may cause you to want to move. We aren't sure why the fire in the tent would cause you to want to leave town, but before you go, we'd like to ask you to stay."

Mom narrowed her eyes. "Why?"

"We've been meaning to come over and talk to you for some time. There are things happening, and we think having you as an ally would benefit us all. You seem like people who would fight on the right side in a battle."

Dad's face pinched. "And what makes you so sure of that?"

Mr. Porter shrugged. "Well, there's Ember. They are an amazing kid. You can't have someone so levelheaded in dealing with such hard issues without good parents. But also from the things Felix has told us."

Mrs. Porter leaned forward. "I think Felix is keeping something from us, something from the trip. You don't have to share—I understand how secrets go—but something happened to spook you, and it wasn't just the misadventure of youth. If you'll trust us, like Felix, we'll fight for your secrets, fight to keep you here."

Dad shook his head. "I don't think you understand. I've spent years protecting my family. We will continue to hide. You knowing our secret just ups what we need to do for our protection."

Felix's hand reached over to clasp Ember's. "So you were right? You and your family will leave? Just disappear? Were you going to say goodbye before you left?"

Mom slumped. "Yes, we were going to leave. And no, saying goodbye opens up too many questions. Ember isn't good at lying ... and telling the truth? It isn't safe, or an option."

Ember turned to their Mom. "I already told you. I can hide my change. No one has to know. I think if we're needed here, we should stay. It's more than just us. We should at least hear them out."

Felix squeezed their hand.

Mom and Dad gazed at each other and then at Felix's parents. Dad said, "If we tell you our secret and it gets out, we can't promise you protection. There are others who have learned our secret. They help us to hide. You wouldn't be the first. We need friends. It's the only way. And as Ember gets older, they will need friends too. But it's dangerous. Knowing us is dangerous."

The Porters briefly looked at each other with a nod, then Mr. Porter said, "We're in. We protect our friends."

Dad nodded then finished his wine. Ember knew they had a few friends that knew, but they'd never been there from the start, when someone was introduced into the fold.

Mom filled Dad's glass, and he took another sip. After a sigh, he started. "Okay. The phoenixes of old are not all extinct. When a prank went poorly in the woods, my child burned to ash. Felix witnessed, not only Ember's death, but their rise from the ashes."

Felix's parents looked at Ember's dad with wide eyes, astonishment and pride beaming from them.

Dad gazed at Ember and Felix. "And what about the two of you, now that you've changed? How does *your boyfriend* feel about you now?" His eyes bore into Felix. "Are you still going to be as enamored with Ember with how they are now?"

Everyone's gazes shifted to him. His parents looked a bit confused. A bright red colored Felix's cheeks, but he straightened in his seat and stared directly into Dad's eyes. "Why would my feelings change? Ember is still Ember and still beautiful."

That shut Dad up for a minute, and the warmth that filled Ember the first time they'd heard that declaration filled them again.

Mrs. Porter turned to Dad, brows still lowered in confusion but apparently unwilling to ask. "There's something else we were hoping to talk to you about. It's something we've been trying to find a time for, but we realize that we've run out of time at this point."

Dad's head tilted. "Oh?"

"I don't know if Ember has told you, but a few times a week, Felix comes home right after school to work with us. We're part of a movement that's been watching Tad Shade. He graduated from a hybrid-college twenty years ago, bottom of his class, a real nobody. The thing is, in college, he started an anti-human club."

Ember leaned forward. "He did what?"

Mom stood and went into the kitchen to find another bottle of wine. When she returned, she handed it to Dad. "I remember him. His strongest magic was void."

Mrs. Porter looked at Mom a bit confused.

Shaking their head, Ember searched the faces of the adults at the table. "A hybrid-college?"

Mr. Porter laughed. "It was a radical idea created some fifty years ago. Put humans and witches together on the same campus, show that they could be trusted to learn together. It took about twenty years for the experiment to fully come to fruition, twenty-five for everyone to realize it was a horrible idea, and thirty for all the hybrid-colleges to close."

Dad's eyes narrowed. "Wait, which college did he attend?"

"Stars Hybrid University, why?" Mrs. Porter looked at Dad with the same warm brown eyes Felix had.

Dad snorted. "Is that the same kid you always complained about, dear? The one who terrorized the campus and was almost kicked out?"

"Expelled, and yes. I was teaching air magic back then, and he would randomly throw void bubbles over the class when he couldn't do what was required. It was obnoxious. When I covered the earth magic class he attended, he did the same thing."

"How did he avoid getting suspended?" Ember was completely invested in the story.

"The other students harassed him. He had evidence and explained his antics were self-defense. Shortly after that, the anti-human club began. I didn't work there much longer after that."

Ember sipped their soda. "So you don't know what happened to him?"

"I don't, hon."

"I do," Mrs. Porter said. "After he left Star Hybrid U, he finally buckled down and studied witch lore. While in college, it never seemed to interest him. His low standings in magic left him working in the human sector. He found a job as a historian and archaeologist at a museum. From what we've figured, he eventually worked his way up to doing some field runs, but most of the others at the museum didn't take his research seriously."

Dad rested his elbow on the table as he munched his pizza. "What type of research did he do? Does anyone know?"

"That's just it. His research was on the forests around the heart of the War of Peace. Most of the time when he went out, he went alone. Then suddenly, ten years ago, he disappeared. When authorities went looking for him, colleagues said a few weeks before he disappeared he kept mumbling about, 'he found it.' No one knew what he'd been talking about or where he went. Five years ago, he reappeared with money and power."

Everyone at the table stared at Mrs. Porter, silent. She shifted her gaze to Dad. "Please, Ash"—she turned to Mom—"Sadie. Consider staying for a little while. Maybe a week or two. Learn about our organization and what we do. This movement Tad has started, it's growing. We're worried where it will go if it isn't contained. We need more people on our side, more people like you. If coming to a meeting or two doesn't convince you, then run. We promise we'll keep your secrets."

Chapter 24 - Duty Calls

Ambrose

Ambrose sat in her room, contemplating the school field trip. Her phone rang. Checking the display, she saw it was Cress. Her shoulders slumped, and she sighed. *Haven't I spent enough time with him this weekend?*

"What do you want, Cress?"

"I just need to talk to someone about how amazing the weekend was, and you're the only one I know who'll understand." His excitement was almost infectious.

"Well, it went as planned. We made names for ourselves, and the accommodations weren't awful."

He scoffed. "Your tent wasn't awful. Josie and I were stuck in the school's tents. I don't know how many palms your dad had to grease to get all the adults to ignore that monstrosity you slept in."

Ambrose smiled to herself. If he knew the magical extras the tent had, he'd be even more annoyed. She'd showered with warm water each morning, unlike everyone else. But there was no way she'd slum it like all the other cretins she went to school with.

She moved to her bed and sat down. "You do know that one of the adults that volunteered to help was a family servant. You've seen him around the house, I'm sure. As soon as we disembarked from the bus, he guided us to the campsite. I didn't say anything because Josie didn't know and she can't keep her mouth shut."

Cress laughed. "She may not be able to shut up, and she's really annoying, but that mud pit was great. She managed to pull that on, what, five groups?"

"Four. That and finding the night plants."

"Yeah, I was wondering about that. Why could your people find the day plants but not the night ones?"

Ambrose sometimes wondered how Cress figured out how to tie his shoes by himself. Hopefully all the pranks would show Ember they didn't belong at the school. Or better yet, prove it to Felix. Then she could have a partner who was worthy of her.

She rubbed the bridge of her nose. "The teachers and adult volunteers were out at night monitoring the finding of the plants, the real assignment. The day plants were extra credit. We could've just hung out in our tents and have been fine. With less scrutiny, there was more freedom for pranks and anyone doing the assignment."

"Oh!" Cress laughed. "That makes sense. You're really smart. Did you know that?"

They'd focused the majority of their pranks on the geeks. The prank they played on Tansy and Olivia went as planned as well. Too bad they'd figured out how to stop the fire so quickly. All in all, they'd hit eight groups. The stories would be passed around the school, growing with each telling. *At least they better!*

I just hate that Felix always calls me out on staff aiding me on my work. It isn't like that's not how the real world works. I could do it if I needed, but why, when I have people to do it for me?

A knock came at her door. "Cress, I have to go. Someone is knocking on my door."

"K, talk to you later."

She hung up before he could say more. The door to her room opened, and her father walked in. He stood tall, shoulders back, with a serious look on his face. He sat in the second chair at her large oak school desk. "Tell me about the weekend. Did you collect all the plants you needed?"

"You know we did. You sent someone to ensure the assignment was completed, regardless of side activities."

"And *were* there distractions?"

Ambrose just sat, staring at her father. That question didn't deserve an answer.

A wicked smile spread across his face. "Were any pranks pulled on you and Cress and that obnoxious girl, or were you three the terrors in the trees?"

Again, she gave him the blank stare the question deserved. She didn't know what had gotten into her father. He wasn't usually this nosy, or social. There was only one issue from the weekend she wanted to address with her father. "I do have a question for you, Father. At one point I wanted to, well, start a fire. My fire magic just, I dunno, fizzled out."

His face morphed from playful to concern. "What do you mean 'fizzled out'? What were you doing at the time?"

"Does that matter?"

"It might."

The muscles in her body tightened. She didn't want to admit to her father she wanted to light Ember's shirt on fire while they were wearing it. She knew that was extreme. But, if that mattered, it mattered. She told her father about the night and the series of pranks she, Cress, and Josie played on Ember.

He rubbed his eyes. "This is Felix's girlfriend?"

"Not girlfriend, it's who he's dating. Gods, Father, you're so old." Father's face scrunched in confusion. "Just, leave it at that."

Father shook his head. "Okay, so Felix is dating Ember. If I remember correctly, there was a time before Cress that you had your sights set on Felix. Smart, cute, or whatever you kids say. Strong in his magic, am I right?"

Ambrose's chin dropped as she gave her father a death stare. She had to stop him from talking.

"So, I'm right. You're picking on this kid, to the point of being willing to burn them, because Felix is an old crush. Maybe your magic didn't work because, deep down, you knew it was wrong and you stopped yourself."

A brow rose on her forehead. "You think I felt guilty or grew a conscience?"

"Do you have a better reason?"

She slumped. "No, not really. And I guess I knew burning Ember's shirt was a bad idea. So yeah, your theory could be correct."

"Don't sound so upset that you made the right decision. If you'd followed through with that, Ambrose, I couldn't have saved you from expulsion."

His words hit her like a bucket of ice-cold water. She turned to dismiss him, and he continued. "You need to change into something ... prettier. Mr. Shade will be joining us for dinner to give you your talking points for this week's assembly."

Ambrose spun to face him. "Why should I even be there. Just get what he wants me to say."

"He prefers it when you're there."

"Father, that's just gross. He's old. I don't need much time to memorize his plans. They're simple. If you really think about it, he's simple too. It's why he wants other people to represent him."

He slapped her across the cheek at her audacity to talk back to him. The sharp pain blossomed across her face and to her soul. He hissed out at her, "Do *not* speak like that. Don't think like that. This man is going to bring about much needed change in our society and then be the leader of the new order created." The light in his eyes proved how much he believed the words he spoke. Ambrose shivered at his zeal. "You'd be lucky if he chose you to be his queen."

Ambrose licked the inside of her lip and tasted blood. She'd never been slapped before. Her parents had always spoiled her. Hands trembling, she pushed away from the desk and headed towards her closet. "Okay, Father. I'll find a dress. Do you know his favorite color?"

"And put on some makeup to cover that bruise."

Chapter 25 - Double Trouble over the Years

Ember

Felix helped Ember clear the table. The two of them cleaned up while the adults continued to talk.

Ember's focus wasn't on the plates of leftover pizza. It was all on this person Mom used to teach, this Mr. Shade. Mrs. Porter continued her story while they cleaned. "It was probably five years ago that he started running an anti-human organization. It started small, but you know there are many magic users upset that humans have equal rights to them and proportional representation in government. Where his club at University failed, in the wild it grew and grew fast."

"People didn't remember him from college," Mr. Porter cut in. "The young thought him a savior come to bring salvation to a cause they didn't even know they wanted. It took about a year before his ramblings caught the attention of our organization."

"And what group is that, exactly?" Mom asked smoothly as she sipped her wine.

He turned and dipped his head at her. "We work for the FB Coalition. It's a private think tank that's been around—"

"We know of it," Mom cut in. Ember turned quickly and saw her face looked blank. Looking at Dad, he stared hard at Felix's parents, as if trying to see into their heads.

Ember didn't know what they knew but was curious to know the full story.

Mr. Porter nodded slowly. "I was hoping you'd heard of us. Not many people know about it. If you've heard of us, that tells me a lot about your standing in the community and that we were right to approach you."

Mom placed her glass on the table. "Approach us about what?"

"We want you to join. Both of you ... all three of you. As Mr. Shade and his group grows, we need more people.

He's recruiting in the schools, as Ember probably told you, and his message is resonating. War is coming, and I don't think anyone can live with their head in the sand. From what Felix tells us, you have moved a lot over the years. Well, in your last move, you landed in Tad Shade's center of action. He's here in town. That's why his assemblies have started in the school."

"Of course we did," Dad grumbled. "Anything that can go wrong or be dangerous naturally falls on us, and with two of us, it's doubly as bad."

The Porters looked at him confused, and he waved it off. Mr. Porter continued. "His biggest push right now is claiming that the humans are trying to start his war. That *they* want to take down the witches."

Ember mumbled, "That's just stupid, but the message is all over school."

All the adults turned to face them. Mrs. Porter smiled. "Yes, Ember, you're correct, and I'm glad you see that. It's unfounded. But if anyone pushes back in a closed situation with these people, they're branded a human lover and laughed out of the meeting."

"I won't come out and tell the world what I am or who my child is. I've kept in hiding since the War of Peace. I've kept Ember a secret since their birth. If we decide to stay, we are all just magic users."

Felix and Ember returned to the table with drinks. Felix tilted his head. "Can I ask a question, Mr. Savita?"

"You can ask, Felix, but the answer is a whole other matter."

Felix laughed. "Right, of course. I've been wondering since I realized what Ember was yesterday. Well, I guess you'd have to know. I've researched phoenixes a lot over the years. Well, researched all shifters." His parents snorted. "They fascinate me. Anyway, in all my research, I learned that phoenixes could only do fire magic, and shapeshifters could only, well ..." His face burned a bright red. "... breed with other shifters of the same type." The last words flew out of him like he'd pushed them out despite himself.

Mom's face transformed with her smile. "Your research hasn't led you down the wrong path, young man. For the most part, you're absolutely correct. Phoenixes are the one shifter that can breed outside of their shifter type. We actually didn't know that before Ember came along."

Mrs. Porter looked up to the ceiling. "So, Ember is good at fire, very good. Too good to be trained at school. From you, Sadie, they get air and earth magic. That makes Ember a full witch with three abilities."

Felix laughed. "Oh no, mom. Ember has–" He slapped his hands over his mouth and looked from Ember to their mom, eyes wide.

Mom shook her head. "Ember's earth magic is weak. You may as well not count it. Their air magic is ..." She looked at Ember as if deciding what to say, then she sighed. "Decent. Fire, brilliant."

"If you evened out Ember's abilities, they would almost pan out to be like any other magic user. Though, their fire may be too good," Dad explained. "But their fire is that of a phoenix. That means, in essence, they are fire. If we knew what a regular fire magic user could do, maybe we could figure out how to dumb down their ability enough to send Ember to classes, but it's hard to tamp it down to that level."

"In class, my air magic is usually good. Having flown in the stuff, I have an appreciation for air that other students don't have. Mom taught me before I started in public school. Her air magic is top-notch. If you could see the stuff she does. I'm already dumbing myself down for that class."

Both their parents looked at them. Mom spoke first. "I knew you were holding back, love, but are you dumbing it down?"

Ember shrugged. "I want to see the different things they have to teach. Some of the skills are interesting. I can do the big, flashy stuff that we've done. If I had shown them my true abilities at the start, they'd have moved me up, and I'd never have learned the basics. Once I was tracked into the class I'm in, moving up didn't seem worth it. Same as potions."

Everyone got silent for a moment, thinking about the logic behind that move.

Finally, Felix leaned in. "And the two of you are the last of your kind, the last two phoenixes, alone in the world?"

Dad looked pained. "I led the armies during the War of Peace. Watching all the phoenixes sacrifice themselves leading the charge almost killed me. There was one other leader. We needed two ... for reasons I may get into later, not now. Once we won, she and I both needed time to decompress. There weren't cell phones or the internet back then. I haven't seen her since."

Shock rocked Ember back. She'd never heard about this other phoenix. "Who, Dad? Who is this other phoenix?"

"My sibling ... my sister ... my twin."

Chapter 26 - A Total Makeover

Ember

Ember gazed at the bags scattered around them. They hated shopping, but it was worth it because they could stay. Their parents said they would stick around as long as Ember could fool people into thinking they hadn't shifted. They'd always liked a good challenge.

Mom didn't seem to mind shopping. They could enter a shop, and the clothes she sought seemed to fly to her. Mom bribed Ember with ice cream in the food court ... after real food, of course.

"Do you think Dad really went in to complain to the school about the antics of the field trip today?"

"I do. You were put in real danger. Not to mention, they burned your clothes while you were bathing. There are a lot of issues with that. I think if they'd stuck to everything *but* that, he'd have ignored it, but leaving you to possibly be naked, running through woods you don't know ... that's one thing too many."

Ember sipped their chocolate malt. "I guess getting a day off has been nice. If nothing else, to decompress. I know we're at the mall, but it's so empty. And we can go home now, and I can sit in my room ... alone?"

"Not quite. We've gotten you some new pants and some tops. Items that will easily blend in with what you wore before. Some undergarments that should hide anything. The last time you had this body was right when you turned fourteen, so it's been awhile. It would be nice for you to really get a bit of practice with the clothes."

"I know, Mom. You keep telling me this. What's the bad news you're hiding from me?"

She slumped. "I think you should wear skirts to school. Jeans will be too tight. The baggier sweat pants are great, but you aren't as curvy as you were. Skirts will be your best option. Not a lot has changed with your body. I know most of your old clothes fit just fine, but ... when

Dad wants to fool people, like before we moved and you had two moms, that was his favorite outfit."

"Gods, that was so long ago. I barely remember having two moms. It was like a year, right? Right after we moved when I was five. And then you two went on vacation, and I stayed with Uncle Tom. That's when he came back as Dad again but had to dress as Mom when he was out of the house. Was that for another year? It was so long ago. He's been Dad ever since."

"Well, he's very careful. You learn to avoid the accidents when you're older. But Ember, he shifted on the move to Maine and was that way for two years. He had to present as female for an additional two years. You had two moms for four years."

"Really? That seems crazy. Time and memories are so weird. That time is such a blur."

Mom just smiled. "Now, about what you'll wear to school."

It was Ember's turn to slump. "I've never worn a skirt to school. Won't that alone be remarked upon? I always wear jeans and a T-shirt. We go away on a field trip, and I return girly?"

"If you wear your normal clothes, it will be harder for you to hide your new body. Not impossible, just harder. Why don't we get you a few skirts, and at home, *in your room alone*, you can try different items on and decide. I just want you to have options."

"Fine." Despite the word, Ember didn't think they'd ever wear the girl selections they were about to buy with their mom.

Once home, Ember threw their new clothes into the washer. After everything had dried, they tried on different outfits, testing how each looked. If they adjusted everything, they could make the jeans work. They hated to admit the skirt was more comfortable, but it looked odd, probably because it wasn't anything they were used to seeing on their body.

Just to be silly, they matched the dark-blue skirt with a light-green V-neck sweater and snapped a picture to send to Daisy. She should be out of classes by now.

OMG! I thought you were sick. You went shopping without me. YOU'RE WEARING A SKIRT. Yes! You have to wear that to school. You look amazing. How did your mom talk you into that? She's magic. I mean, she is magic, but OMG!!!

Ember could hear their friend's exuberance. It was one of their favorite things about Daisy.

Several of my outfits got ruined on the outing. Mom wanted me to branch out. I don't know about this. Still thinking.

Daisy sent a heart-eyed emoji. Less think, more wearing that to school. The others will poop bricks. An army of poop emojis followed.

Laughing, Ember flopped on their bed. Not tomorrow, air magic class. Skirts don't mesh well with that class. But, again, it's an option for the future.

Fine! Daisy's exasperation emanated from the one word.

"Ember, dinner in five minutes."

Gotta go, dinner.

Tomorrow then, and Wednesday, Ember in a skirt!

Ember shook their head and tossed their phone on the bed. They quickly changed back into the clothes they'd gone shopping in.

They thought about the reactions of the other students if they wore a skirt. Most wouldn't care, but Josie, Ambrose, and Cress. *Gah, they'd have a field day with it!*

Chapter 27 - Head in the Clouds

Ember

As Ember walked to school, they were glad they'd bought slightly larger jeans the day before. They'd never had a large chest, so it didn't take much padding to make them look mostly the same.

Felix caught up with them outside of school. "Wow, you really look like yourself. If I didn't know, I wouldn't know. That's amazing."

"All my mom. She knows what she's doing. I guess living with Dad all these years has given her some tricks."

He leaned over and kissed Ember's cheek. "Well, I think you're lovely either way. I wish you could be you however you wanted to be."

They smiled. "This is fine. I mostly feel like I did last week. Only a few differences."

Once they got inside, Daisy ran up. "I really wanted you to wear the skirt today. I knew you said you wouldn't, but it would've been epic!"

Felix had been rubbing Ember's back, but his hand froze. "A skirt? You may wear a skirt?" He leaned in closer to their ear. "I take it all back. I may like things better now. That sounds sexy."

Ember pushed him away. "You're both awful. I may burn the damn thing, and you'll never see it."

Trying to be helpful, Daisy pulled up the picture and showed Felix.

"With friends like these," Ember mumbled.

Felix winked. "See you two in Magical History. Have fun in first period."

For eleventh year students, magic lessons were every other day first period and fourth period. Since Ember didn't have a third magical studies class, they took Magical Creations as an elective.

Mrs. Vintl, the teacher, walked to the center of the room. "Okay, everyone, today we're going to start with a basic warm-up. I would like you to create a small twister at the edge of the far wall and have it travel the short length. Follow the easy path today. I want to get to the lesson."

They each turned to the far end. There were colored circles along the wall, and over the years, they'd gotten used to the color they each used. That way what they did wouldn't bump or interrupt each other.

Ember glanced at the green circle, spun their finger, then waved their hand in the direction they wanted the twister to go. The twister was small, maybe six inches tall. The point was control over air. It moved smoothly to the other side. With a flick of their hand to an open-fingered stop sign, their magic dissipated.

A few seconds later, the others finished with their warm-ups.

"Excellent. I didn't think that would be much of a challenge for any of you. Okay, here is our next project. If you notice, there are square wood platforms set around the floor. I would like you each to go sit cross-legged on one."

Again, Ember chose the green one. To their left, Daisy sat on the red platform, and Simon selected the blue one. The tenth year students chose pink, purple, orange, brown, and yellow platforms.

"We're going to begin with a baseline. I would like you all to close your eyes. This way I can get a feeling for what you can do."

Ember closed their eyes. This wasn't anything new. Too many distractions could stop up the works and cause a magic user to falter in a skill they may actually have.

"There are handholds next to where each of you are sitting. Please grab on. I'm going to remind you, despite any sound you may hear, keep your eyes closed until I tell you to open them. Now, feel the air around you. Get a feel for the flow and density of the particles surrounding you. Keeping your eyes shut, everyone. Good, now, I'd like you to bring the flow under your platform, make those particles thick, and lift the wood planks up as high as you can."

Ember smiled. They'd played this game with their mom a few years before coming to Feniks Secondary School. They started off with lifting their platforms. Then, they'd move slowly around the field. It took a while for Ember to really feel comfortable moving themselves by moving the air below the planks they sat on.

At first, the platform had tilted, and Ember took several tumbles. They remembered being battered and bruised a lot during those days, but once they figured out how to push at the corners of what they sat on and not in the center, things began to work much better.

Eventually, they got to the point that they could easily move through the air by manipulating the airstreams under and around where they sat. Then, Mom challenged them to play catch. Ember had collapsed a few times, falling to the ground. Their first games of tossing the ball, they'd kept everything a few feet off the ground. By the end, Ember could almost soar as well with the wood as in bird form.

They both were considering moving to using Ember's body instead of a static platform when Ember had had their last accident, shifted, and ended up in public school. Ember wanted to meet people their own age, and Mom was busy at work. They both prioritized other magics when they did study together. Their private air magic lessons had ended. Ember had forgotten how much they'd missed floating on a platform.

A gasp brought them back to the present. Eyes flying open, Ember realized they'd floated to the ceiling of the room. Slowly, ever so slowly, Ember brought their green plank of wood back to the floor. Staring at Mrs. Vintl's wide eyes, they raised their arms to the sides and shrugged.

Chapter 28 - An Uplifting Distraction

Daisy

Eyes squeezed shut, Daisy attempted to pull the air from around her and push it under her platform. This exercise confused her. She knew that she could lift a sheet of paper and maybe a pencil, but she'd never been able to lift a book with air. She could help support something she wanted to carry, like the log in the woods, but lifting alone was something else.

The class had discussed the density of air before, but this seemed impossible.

She made fists and tensed her muscles. She really wanted to figure this out. *Is it possible, can an air witch fly? Can I fly? That would be, like, the coolest thing ever. Ember and I could fly around the jerks and just laugh at them for being stuck to the ground.* She imagined the two of them, colorful mist flowing from them, flying around the school, avenging all the people Ambrose, Cress, and especially Josie teased and picked on.

With another push of her power, she gave it her all, but nothing happened. She didn't think it was actually possible. It was too bad. It would've been really cool. Then again, why would Mrs. Vintl assign this if it *weren't* possible? Maybe ...

Daisy heard a gasp, but didn't open her eyes. She knew the rules, not until she was told. She really wanted to. If there'd been a crash, she would've, but a small gasp probably meant Simon made his platform wiggle, the jerk. He'd lord it over her and Ember later. "Look how amazing I am. Too bad you two aren't as smart or good as me. I'm just the best in the world, blah blah blah." He annoyed Daisy, but she wouldn't let it ruin her day.

"Okay, class, I think I have your base abilities in this skill set." Daisy opened her eyes and saw the teacher with pen and pad in hand. "I can work with what I saw to create individual lesson plans for each of you." Mrs. Vintl's voice wasn't as chipper as normal, but she was writing in a notebook, so she was probably distracted. "Why don't you collect the platforms and lean them against the wall for me, and then we'll call it good for today."

Daisy took out her phone and checked the display. There were thirty more minutes of class. Mrs. Vintl never ended class early. Daisy raised her hand. At a nod, she asked, "Are you sure? We only get to practice twice a week."

Mrs. Vintl rubbed her eyes and checked her watch. "Of course, you're right. I'm sorry, class. I'm just distracted. My mistake. Once the platforms are stored, there are bricks. If you could place them on their sides and put a notebook across them, you can begin trying to lift the notebook."

"One more question. Is this possible, with the platforms? I've never seen an air witch fly before." Daisy's insides were a jumble of hope and excitement.

A small smile played across Mrs. Vintl's face. "It is. It's very advanced. I like to play around with the theory, though less than five percent of air magic users can master this type of magic. It's a fun exercise, though."

Daisy shimmied with happiness, though a few of the tenth years groaned. Air wasn't her best magical ability—that would be earth—but she wanted to be great at all three of her proficiencies. She sat next to Ember, and her friend watched as she went first. This was normal. Ember looked up to Daisy in air magic, learning from her.

Sitting up taller, Daisy took a breath and again tried to gather the density of airstreams under the notebook. She furrowed her brow and held up her hands. With a strong push, the notebook wiggled then floated up an inch. Daisy squealed, and it fell, landing on the floor. "Yes! Did you see that, Ember? I got the notebook to levitate. That was so cool. I've gotten things to sway in a breeze, but this moved with the density of air I gathered under it."

Ember gave Daisy one of their rare smiles. It wasn't that Ember didn't smile, but this one lit up their whole face. "That's amazing, Daisy. Okay, my turn."

Daisy watched as Ember set up their own notebook on the bricks. They bit their lower lip while focusing on the space just between the pillars. Eyes narrowed, Ember's breathing slowed as they focused. Daisy could feel the air currents shift and move. She even saw the notebook shift, but it didn't even teeter from the bricks.

Finally, after a few minutes, Ember slumped and shrugged. "Oh well, something to practice, I guess."

Daisy gave her friend a big smile. "Absolutely, you'll get there. I'm sure in the next few weeks we'll all figure this next bit out."

They went back and forth, practicing making the air denser under their notebooks. Daisy explained to Ember what she did, hoping to help her friend out. By the end of class, they could both float the notebook off the bricks for a few seconds. They saw Simon, sitting a few feet away, working hard to keep pace with them. His face scrunched up, and he got his notebook floating for almost a minute before it fell back to the floor.

There were a few others who got the notebook to float and a couple whose notebooks stayed glued to the bricks. Obviously, it would take some practice to get everyone to be able to float their full platforms.

They packed up their things and put the bricks into a cupboard. As they moved to the door, Mrs. Vintl said, "Ember, if you don't mind, I'd like to speak with you at the end of the day. I know you're busy until then. You aren't in trouble, just a few minutes of your time."

Daisy shot her friend a quick look. Ember's eyes were closed as they nodded. "Sounds good, Mrs. Vintl. See you then."

As they walked to Magical History, Ember looked pensive. Their shoulders were slumped, and their face was drawn. It was the same look as in the forest after the first tent burned down. They'd had a few bad days. "You okay? Do you think you're in trouble?"

"What?" Ember shook their head and focused on Daisy. "Trouble? Oh, with Mrs. Vintl? No, probably not. She saw me struggling where you and Simon picked it up quickly. She probably just wants to give me some pointers without embarrassing me. It's fine for the tenth years to be behind, but we eleventh years need to be the leaders."

Daisy thought about it and decided that made sense. Mrs. Vintl was nothing if not really nice. She'd never do anything to embarrass a student.

Chapter 29 - As Things Go from Bad to Worse

Ember

Ember dropped into their seat in Magical History. They couldn't believe the mistake they made. It was like mistakes were following them around. First the spatial magic, then being outed as a phoenix. Only to Felix and his family, but still, in their seventeen years, it was the first time it'd happened, and now this.

They knew the power of bad luck and phoenixes, but this was ridiculous.

They knew to be careful with what they did in air magic class. Yet, the memory of a game they hadn't played in years was their undoing. It had been too long since Ember had been in the air. It wasn't an excuse, but they knew it was part of it. When they got home tonight, they'd ask Dad to take them out flying.

Felix came in, and with one look, his face morphed from happy to concerned. "Everything okay?"

"Yeah, I just did something stupid last class. I'll try to fix it after school, but explaining it to my parents will be like dinner Sunday night: awkward and uncomfortable."

His eyes widened. "It can't be as bad as all that, Ember, can it?"

They realized he must think they were talking about phoenixes. Ember shook their head. "I messed up in air magic class. I'll explain later."

Felix's body relaxed as he realized the probable degree of bad they meant. "Okay, good. We'll talk about it later."

Mr. Elias stood from behind his desk. "Today, we're going to begin our discussion of the aftermath of the War of Peace. But first, a twenty minute write-up on the historical significance of collecting plants at night. We're magic users. Why do we need to mix spells?"

There were grumbles, but people got out paper and started to write. Mr. Elias circled the room as everyone did what he asked. Once the time was up, he took the time to collect the papers.

"Excellent, now on to war!" His eyes shone. "The battles were fought, we'd lost our shifters, humans now knew about magic users and people who could shift into animals ... now what?"

Cress raised his hand, leaning back with a smirk on his face. After getting called on, he said, "We bent over—all the magic users, that is—taking it from behind, allowing the humans to believe they held some weird equality to superior beings."

Students all over the class laughed at his summary. Mr. Elias held up a hand. "As cute as that was, it was also inappropriate. Unless you want detention, you'll keep all your answers classroom appropriate. If you study history, the winners and the losers all agreed the final outcome brought a tranquility to the land. The humans had just learned about magic users, and it took time for that to really register with the general population. New laws were put in place to help with the integration of the two very different groups and to aid in their cohabitation."

Josie laughed. "Did the two groups ever cohabitate?"

Felix turned to her. "If you spent more time studying and less time being a bully, maybe you'd know that answer. Yes, not only did we have two hundred years of everyone getting along, there have been sections of our history when communities were intermixed, including the schools. Even today, there are many jobs where humans and magic users work together, not to mention within our legislature. Are you really so simpleminded?"

Josie huffed and turned back towards the front. Ambrose, looking like she'd eaten a lemon, pursed her lips. Then she smiled at Felix. "As always, you're right. Ever the smart one, Felix. The thing is, as much congeniality as we've faced for the last two hundred years, it doesn't change the fact that in the last few years, things have changed. It started with a few malcontented humans, but it is something we have to be concerned with."

"Stop." Mr. Elias's voice was harder than Ember had ever heard it. "We are focusing on events of two hundred years ago. I refuse to have you spout your families talking points in class, Ambrose. You had an assembly last week, and if I'm not mistaken, you have another one this week. We will not spend any of *my* class discussing this."

Ambrose slowly turned to face the front of the room, face reddening. "Sorry, Mr. Elias. Two hundred years ago, the magic users and the humans created a coalition of ten to create legislation that would ensure the peace between them. There were five magic users and five humans. The ten were led by the leaders of the magic users. Now, this is where I get confused. In many of the writings, the leaders were two phoenixes. But in other writings, all the phoenixes sacrificed themselves. I have a journal that explains that the top leaders, a brother and sister phoenix pair, survived the battle. If that's the case, not all of the phoenixes died out. So, was there a phoenix in this coalition? They began a year after the war ended, once the humans were ready to really sit down and work things out. The talks took an additional six months. Many of the laws we think of as being natural to our day-to-day life were created in those discussions. Should I list any of them out, sir?"

Tansy spoke up. "Is it true that there were schools that had both humans and witches?"

"Why?" Josie asked with a sneer. "Do you love non-magic users? Are you a human lover? People like Ember?"

Ember sighed. "The most recent colleges that were hybrid-schools were closed twenty-some odd years ago. But, if you read the books, there were lower-level elementary schools with mixed populations throughout the two hundred years."

"It's true," Mr. Elias said. "Some communities, even today, aren't big enough for two school systems. Parents are then responsible for the magical education of their kids. Until secondary school, we figure it's okay."

Cress leaned towards Ember, eyes alight with mischief. "Is that what happened to you? Stuck with only your parents to teach you until you came here? Is that why you're so magically stunted? I'm starting to feel bad for you. Stuck with humans, your parents your only teachers, obviously sucky ones. Poor baby Ember."

Ambrose turned her head to them. "Who *is* your mom, anyway? I know your dad isn't anyone with the last name Savita."

Ember ignored her, but Felix sighed. "You are so worried about who's who in the magical community. You don't know everyone, Ambrose. Why would the name Sadie Savita mean anything to you, anyway?"

Ambrose flipped her black hair. "It doesn't, and that's the point."

Mr. Elias made a small gasping sound. Ember shifted their gaze from Ambrose to him. He stared at Ember, mouth slightly open. He snapped it closed. "Okay, everyone, we have another minute before class ends. Ember, you missed class yesterday. If you could come to my class during one of my off hours or after school, I'll get you caught up with what you missed."

Before they could respond, the bell rang.

Two classes, two requests for their presence after school. Today was turning out to be a real doozy of a day.

Chapter 30 - Layers of Secrets

Ember

Ember decided to branch out and get a cheese bagel and fries for lunch. *Nothing but healthy food for me!* Something about the bagel toasted with three different cheeses soothed anyone on a bad day.

They made it to the corner table without running into any of the mean crowd. Felix and Daisy sat eating when they arrived.

"And then I got to show Ember my technique. It was pretty stellar. How about your morning classes?"

Felix smiled as Ember took the seat next to him. "Mine were fine. Mind magic. Starting my day with Cress every day for two classes in a row is always a treat. Though, he's remarkably better when neither Josie nor Ambrose are around."

"So, did Ember tell you that two teachers want to see them after school today?" Daisy winked as she sipped her soda.

Felix faced them. "Air magic?"

"Yeah, she wants to see me after classes. And, before you ask, I don't know why."

Daisy bounced. "I'm sure you—"

Simon placed his tray at their table, joining them. "Hi."

Felix's eyes narrowed. "Simon."

"What are you doing here?" Daisy asked. "Don't you usually sit ... actually, I don't know where you usually sit."

"I usually work in the library during lunch, but there's a meeting going on, and the librarian asked that I come to the cafeteria. I wasn't sure where to sit but figured you all wouldn't be awful to socialize with."

Ember snorted. "Such praise. Thanks."

He shrugged. "So, you got in trouble in class. What did you do? Fail bad enough to need special tutoring? Did you cheat?"

"What is it with your obsession with cheating? Maybe Mrs. Vintl just wants to make sure I'm okay after missing school yesterday."

Simon's head tipped to the left. "You weren't here yesterday? Huh, who knew. But I doubt she would've known. You probably messed up to the point she feels you need extra personal help. I mean, everyone in school knows you don't have much power. Outside of air magic, do you even show any power?"

"Did you really come over and join us to be a jerk? Lunch is our time to relax and have a good time. If you're really here to put me down, you can just leave." Ember didn't need to take his criticism.

"What did I say?" Simon looked baffled.

Daisy squinted at him. "Are you simple, Simon? You literally came over here and started spouting insults. Has no one taught you in seventeen years how to be a decent person?"

He blushed. "Sorry, Daisy."

"It isn't me you should be apologizing to." She made a disapproving face at him.

"Oh, yeah, right. Sorry, Ember."

Ember sighed. "Whatever, I accept your apology."

They spent a few minutes eating in relative silence. Finally, Simon asked, "So, do you two think this new challenge Mrs. Vintl gave us is actually possible?"

Ember stared at him, face blank. They weren't sure how secret they should keep their magical ability. It had been awhile since they'd really talked to their parents. Maybe it was time for a conversation. "It's possible."

Everyone looked at them. Daisy narrowed their eyes. "You seem so sure."

"I am. It's possible."

The bell rang before they could ask them anything else.

"Come on, Ember!" Daisy said. "Gym class."

Ember froze. *How could I have forgotten gym class? I am not prepared.* "I'll meet you there."

Daisy's brows came together, but she nodded, grabbed her bag, and left.

Ember took out their phone and sent a text to their dad. `I'm not prepared for gym. What do I do?`

His reply came quickly. `Go to the office. Tell them you're feeling queasy. Call me, I'll get you out of class today. We'll figure it out for tomorrow.`

After Dad made the call, Ember convinced the office to let them go to Mr. Elias's classroom to sit. He had the period free, and they could sit and have downtime. After Dad had yelled at the administration, they were apprehensive to say 'no.'

When Ember got to their Magical History class, the door was cracked open. They knocked and heard a soft, "Come in."

Ember pushed the door and stepped in.

Mr. Elias sat at his desk behind a stack of papers. "Ember, don't you have class right now?"

"I wasn't feeling up to gym. Instead of sitting in the office, I thought I could sit here, if that's okay with you."

"Sure. And then we can talk, and you don't have to come here after school." "Since you were the second teacher to request that, it would be nice to get one out of the way."

His brow rose. "A popular student today?"

They shrugged.

He came around his desk and sat in one of the student desks next to them. "Can I ask you about your family?"

Ember clenched their jaw but tried to keep a blank face. "I guess."

"As you know, I've studied history. It has been my specialty since I went to college. My focus was on the War of Peace, the players, and the fallout. I've spent my life studying everything I could on that war. To be honest, one event that combines the loss of so many of our people, the outing of magic to humans, and their eventual acclimations, and the peace that followed ... it's all fascinating."

Ember wasn't sure where he was going with this. They'd just learned her dad ... and his twin had been big players in the last war, but what did that have to do with their mom, a magic user? Why did her name cause a teacher to want to see them after school?

"I know all that, Mr. Elias. I love hearing you speak about history. You bring it to life with everything you know."

"Probably similar to your parents bringing it to life?"

"My parents?"

He stood, went over to his desk, and grabbed a piece of paper. When he sat back down, he placed the paper upside down on his desk. "I usually teach today's lesson a bit differently. As annoying as Ambrose can be in her arrogant interruptions, today's snobbery may have been a blessing in disguise. Part of the lesson I assign to the class some years is learning the names of the ten members of the coalition that brokered peace. It isn't a common practice, but it's something I like to do."

Ember tilted their head. "So you don't do it every year?"

"No, maybe once every three or four years when I have a student who seems especially interested. Since Felix is so knowledgeable of the war, I was going to include it this year." He held the paper up, about to hand it to Ember. "Here are the names of the five people from each side who ensured our country ran smoothly for the last two hundred years. These names aren't really known in our community since it's not taught. I think after their contribution, the members requested their names not be highlighted. They wanted the laws to be important, not them. Few historians besides me have done the research to learn who they were." He finally handed the paper over.

Ember took the sheet and read over the names. The first five were the human contingent. The names didn't register as anything much. Then they got to the magic users. The second name on the list was Ash Savita, the fourth was Sadie Savita.

Mouth dry, Ember gazed at their parents' names on a list of people who brokered peace two hundred years ago. It didn't surprise them to see their dad's name, but their mom's? How could she be on the list? It didn't make any sense. She couldn't be that old.

Licking their lips, they finally took a breath of air. Their hand fell to the desktop, and they lifted their focus to a teacher who may have figured out more about them than was safe.

"Is there any chance I could speak with your parents, Ember? I understand if they don't feel comfortable or if they want to keep their identities on the down-low. That's why I didn't teach this list this year, and I won't next year either. But, to be honest, the idea of meeting them blows my mind."

They shook their head. "I don't know, sir. All I can do is ask."

Chapter 31 - Decision Made

Ember

"Escribe la tarea en sus notas." La maestra tocó la pizarra ... Ember shook their head. The teacher tapped the board to emphasize the assignment she wanted written down. The bell rang as Ember got the last of the details down.

Daisy waited for them in the hall. "Okay, classes are done. Wanna come over today?"

"Yes, I really do. I can't, but I do. Maybe tomorrow? I have to go see Mrs. Vintl, and then my parents texted me about missing gym and two teachers who wanted to talk to me."

"Gah, good luck with that! Yeah, gym. You never did 'see me soon' like you promised. What happened?"

"I must've eaten something, maybe all that cheese. My stomach didn't feel good. I called Dad. He said to just sit it out today. I ended up going to see Mr. Elias. He told me about yesterday's class. One fewer appointment."

Daisy gave Ember a quick hug. "Good luck. I'll see you tomorrow. Text me tonight and let me know how things went."

Guilt niggled at Ember at the lies they kept telling Daisy as they trudged up the stairs to Mrs. Vintl's office. By the time they got up to the top , their legs were tired. Ember stopped at the door, nerves alight with the knowledge this conversation could change everything. *Can I convince Mrs. Vintl to ignore everything she saw this morning?*

The large room was empty, so they crossed to the small room on the far side and knocked.

"Enter."

Ember opened the door. The office was small with a wooden desk pushed against the left-side wall. There were papers surrounding a laptop that looked like it was drowning. Mrs. Vintl sat in a chair, and a second chair sat open next to her.

"Ember, thanks for returning. Shut the door, and please have a seat. This should be a quick discussion."

Nodding, Ember did as asked.

Mrs. Vintl organized a few of the papers before she turned to face them. "Since you joined my class, I felt you may be holding back. Your abilities aren't consistent. Some days you do well, some days you flop, but the fails seem very contrived. Today I saw the beginning of what you really can do."

She stopped talking and waited, as if hoping Ember would fill in. After a few moments she gave a curt nod. "Right. So, first question, why do you hold back in class?"

Ember lifted their shoulders up to their ears. "I guess it's just habit at this point. I've spent my whole time at this school trying to blend in."

Mrs. Vintl laughed. "Dear, I don't think blending is in your nature. Most people in this school know of the student who doesn't do magic despite going to magic school. If you really wanted to blend in, can I suggest start doing magic? It may help your cause."

A blush climbed Ember's cheeks, warming their face. "I guess I never thought about that. I started off in this class wanting to learn the basics. I know most of the advanced stuff already."

"So you *have* done what we did today before."

"Yeah, Mom and I used to play catch zooming about on platforms."

Mrs. Vintl blanched. "You did what? And at what age? My goodness, you really have been holding back. I'd love to know the real extent of what you can do, maybe meet this mom of yours and figure out a real training schedule for you." Her eyes narrowed at the shock in Ember's face. "This is a school. We're here to teach you, challenge you, help you grow as a person and a witch. We can only do that if we know what you can do and give you new goals that stretch your abilities."

Ember slumped. "Yeah, okay, I'll speak with my parents tonight, see what they have to say."

"Thank you. Here's my personal cell phone number. I know that isn't standard, but if they have any questions or want to keep your abilities under wraps, have them call or text me. Maybe we can figure something out so that you're being challenged without everyone here knowing about it."

Ember nodded, took the number, and stood. The list of triggers they had to present to their parents tonight kept growing. They didn't know if running hadn't been the right choice after all.

Their bag hit the floor as they landed on the couch, face-planting into a pillow. They heard their parents moving around the house, but they wanted a few minutes to decompress from the day. They figured after talking about everything, Mom and Dad would need a few minutes as well.

"How was your day, honey?"

"Delightful."

"Oh no! Was it that bad? Did the clothes not work?" Mom came in and sat on one of the chairs that flanked the couch.

"No, the outfit worked great. No one suspected a thing. People won't look for what they don't expect. We forgot about gym, though. I have to figure out an outfit and where to change."

Mom groaned. "Damn it, I knew there was something niggling at the back of my mind. You normally wear a tank top and shorts. The shorts should work, but a black T-shirt would be better. I'll grab one of your dad's."

Ember pushed themself up. "That should work. I'll change in the bathroom. I don't think anyone will care."

"Was that it? Gym?"

"No, but I think Dad should be here for the rest."

Once both parents were present, Ember pulled out the page from Magical History. "Mr. Elias didn't teach this today. He said he wouldn't teach it this year or next, but he's kind of geeking out. He wants to meet the two of you, if you're willing."

Mom took the page and read it over with a sigh. "This hasn't popped up in a few years. Is this going to be a problem?" She passed it over to Dad, who grumbled.

"He said he wouldn't tell anyone, so I don't think so."

Dad crumpled the paper. "If I'd have known the hassle that committee had been, I'd have told the president to shove it. Find Nuri, and give her the job. She was always better with such things."

Mom smiled at him warmly. "You would've done no such thing. Your sister was good, but you were the leader of the magical forces. You had to be there. I was the only person on that list who could've said no."

"Nope, if you weren't there, I would've walked."

Ember shook their head, a headache starting to pound. "Mom, how were you even there? Witches aren't long-lived."

Their parents looked at each other, then at Ember. "When a phoenix makes a commitment to another being, if they do a real commitment ceremony, their life partner gets a bit of the phoenix immortality. There is a lot of phoenix lore you don't know yet, hon. We've been waiting until you reach the right age. That is also part of the lore. In the world of phoenixes, you are still very young."

Ember rubbed their temples. "So, wait, you're telling me you're over two hundred years old? I mean, I knew Dad was like a bazillion years old."

"Something like that," Mom said with a chuckle.

Dad rubbed his eyes. Apparently, Ember wasn't the only one ready to end this conversation. "Is that it for your day?"

"Well, no." They explained everything that happened with Mrs. Vintl, both in class and after school. They handed the piece of paper with the teacher's number to their mom.

Their parents sat gazing at them for a few minutes, the tension rising. Finally, Mom nodded. "I think this teacher is right," she said in a decisive tone. "You should start doing more with air magic. Forget trying to hide your abilities. You know the basics. It's time for you to shine, my firebird. We'll still keep the fire magic hidden, but you can become the best air witch that school has ever seen."

The glint in their mom's eyes kind of scared Ember.

Chapter 32 – Parent-Teacher Conference

Ember

Wednesday morning, Ember decided to wear a skirt. The black skirt went to just above their knees. They paired it with a gray button-down. They didn't know if they'd go for showing their magic today, but if something arose, they wouldn't hold back.

They were up early, so they made a lunch for school— it always tasted better—then they wouldn't have to wait in line at lunch. Then they made breakfast. They ate quickly before heading out.

As they walked the school halls, they tried not to think about how cold their legs felt. This was going to be a whole new experience.

A tackle came from behind. "Oh my god! I can't believe you did it! You look amazing. Felix is going to be gob smacked when he sees you. This day will be epic!"

Ember wasn't sure how Daisy could get so many words in such a small amount of space. "I don't know how epic it will be. It's an outfit. But we'll see how today goes."

Felix walked up. "Very nice. I hope this isn't a one-time thing."

"Maybe. Let's just get to class. We'll see how today pans out before any final decisions are made."

They made it to earth magic class. Josie scrunched her nose. "What is wrong with you? Tired of looking like a pauper human?"

Tansy stepped up. "I dunno. I think you look nice."

"Whatever!" Josie rolled her eyes and spun, walking away.

The teacher came out. "Okay, today we're going to do a skill-drill. We will search for rocks in a square foot of land and pull them up to the surface. This is a practice of precision and patience."

Ember moved over to Felix and spoke low. They had an idea of how they could finally participate, but they knew it would be a bit of a cheat. *Maybe all Simon's claims of me cheating have finally taken over.*

Class started, and Ember mentally probed the area they were assigned. It was one of the few earth magic skills they actually had. After a few minutes, they found a rock. Sweat gathered on their back and they were breathing hard, but they were determined to be successful in class.

Mrs. Vintl had been correct. To blend in, Ember had to do magic.

Searching a bit lower, Ember found dirt. With a small growl, they started the process again. It took finding four rocks before they found one with a small hole in the dirt beneath it. They sent a mental 'thank you' to Felix. They tapped into the air magic and made the air denser. They may not have been able to move a rock up using earth magic, but a dense ball of air was another matter altogether.

It took time, but eventually, the rock broke through. Ember picked it up, putting it on their tray. A giddy feeling bubbled within them, and they started the process all over again. This time, they searched for the air bubbles instead of the rocks.

By the end of class, Ember's head throbbed. Searching the soil wasn't easy. They also had a pile of six stones. Others in the class had many more, but six was respectable. Josie sauntered over, a smirk on her face. Ember waited for her smart remark. When she saw the pile, her jaw dropped. "Did you actually call up six rocks? By yourself? Holy hell! Ember did magic!" Her shock was enough that the statement sounded genuine.

Felix came over and threw his arm over Ember's shoulder. "Let it go, Josie. Just because you don't know what they can do, doesn't mean they can't do it."

Josie still mumbled about Ember doing magic at the start of second period. They wanted to slap the girl. They began to wonder if it was worth it. *It'll be worth it in the end if I just become another magic user. All three of them will start to ignore me ... hopefully.*

Class started, but before Mr. Elias could start his lesson, Felix raised his hand. "I know we talked about this last week, but I did some research, and I wanted to ask about spatial magic again. Not about why we aren't teaching it, but ... well, could the proficiency still be around?"

Cress guffawed ... again. "Are you kidding me? We're wasting valuable class time discussing this nut-shop topic."

Felix sighed. "It's literally magical history, nitwit. Not to mention, it was a proficiency that helped cinch the winning of the War of Peace, something we're studying now, that theoretically doesn't exist now. So, it's relevant to the lesson. Again, study more. One day, you'll have to tie your own shoes."

There were chuckles around the class at that.

Cress leaned forward and looked ready to pounce, but Mr. Elias put up his hands. "Enough, both of you. In all honesty, if I were to guess, there could be witches with this proficiency out there today. If there are, my guess is there's fewer than a dozen."

Ambrose raised her hand but started speaking before she was called on. "If someone had such an amazing power, why wouldn't the witch be yelling it from the tallest building, bragging and being proud of their unique skill?"

Josie pumped her fist in the air. "Totally!"

Ember thought they saw a muscle in Mr. Elias's jaw twitching as his chest and shoulders rose and fell with a deep breath. "If it were me, I may not want to brag about something everyone in our community is so obsessed with. A lost proficiency. Some are studying why it disappeared and if they can recreate it. It's unique enough that anyone manifesting the power would be studied. Their life would cease to be their own."

It took a few minutes, but Ember saw as realization spread through the class. The idea of being studied scared many people.

As always, the rest of the day smoothed out once she stopped sharing classes with the terrible trio. A few students remarked on Ember's skirt, but beyond that, it was school as usual. After Spanish class, Ember made their way back to Magical History for the meeting with Mr. Elias and their parents. They started feeling like it was their classroom of the week.

They were walking down the hall when they saw their parents walking towards them. "Where are we going, Ember?" Dad's voice shot out.

Mom smiled. "You look lovely in that outfit, dear. I hope it was worth branching out for."

They shrugged and hugged their mom.

"Which door, Ember?" Dad asked again.

"This one," they said, turning to the one they all stood in front of. Ember knocked.

"Come in."

The door swung open to an empty room, save Mr. Elias sitting at his desk, grading papers. Ember immediately went and sat at their normal desk. Their parents went to Mr. Elias and shook his hand.

"Hi, Mr. Elias. I'm Sadie Savita. It's a pleasure to meet you."

"Mrs. Savita, no, really, the pleasure is all mine. And"—it looked to Ember like it took a force of will to shift his gaze from Mom to Dad—"Mr. Savita."

Dad gave a slight nod. "Ember tells us you have studied the last war, the War of Peace, and wanted to meet us. I think that's interesting, but I'm not sure why."

Mr. Elias's face lost all its color. "I ... I don't want to presume. I've been researching the War of Peace since I was Ember's age. The battle, the information suddenly available to the humans, the years it took for the integration of the two societies. I've gone on pilgrimages to different libraries to find journals and, well, anything I could find. There are some key pieces from the battle that are lost to the common lore currently passed down in the history books."

"And do you teach those key pieces?" Dad asked softly. The question may have sounded innocent, but Ember could hear the stress in Dad's question.

Mr. Elias smiled. "Sometimes. Not in this class or any of my general Magical History classes, but at times I have a student who has a similar interest to the topic to me. They ask for an independent Magical History class focusing on the War of Peace. To be honest, I'm expecting Ember's boyfriend, Felix, to request it next year. It happens about once every three to five years. I usually allow those students to guide their studies based on interests, and if their research flows into those key areas, yes, I'll teach it to them."

The tension in Dad's neck and shoulders told Ember he wasn't happy with the answer. In all honesty, it could have been worse. Then again, they didn't know what the key pieces of information were.

"What are some of those fun facts you've taught our bright scholars?" Mom asked, deflecting from Dad.

Mr. Elias gazed between Mom and Dad, his mouth opening and closing as if he couldn't bring himself to say more. Finally, he shook his head. "The armies were led by phoenixes."

Mom gave him a warm smile. "That's in all the history books."

"But, there were two main generals who led the troops, and they weren't in the fray. Those two weren't part of the sacrifices."

Ice formed within Ember, starting at their shoulders and flowing down their back. Cold and unyielding. This is what Ambrose hinted at, but Mr. Elias didn't confirm. *What does he know?*

Dad relaxed. "Are you saying that there are phoenixes in the world?"

Ember's teacher stood a bit taller. "What I'm saying, Mr. Savita, is I have a list of people who helped broker peace two hundred years ago, and your name is on the list."

Dad visibly relaxed and gave Ember's teacher a smile he'd give a small child. "It's a family name, nothing more."

"And your wife?"

"That's a funny story. We didn't even realize the coincidence until our fourth anniversary. It was my cousin, who, like you, is obsessed."

Mr. Elias's head tilted to the side, less sure. "A coincidence?"

Mom's smile widened. "Unless you think a magic user like myself could be two hundred years old." She held out her hand and created a small twister in the center. "Catch, Ember!" She threw the thing.

Ember caught it, picking up the wind spirals, and let the thing climb up and down their arm.

Turning back to Mr. Elias while he watched Ember, Mom said, "As you can see, even Ember can use magic. A phoenix can only do fire from what I remember from my studies. It *had* been some years since I did any reading on those shifters. Then there's the very well-known fact that shifters can only breed with shifters."

Mr. Elias continued to watch Ember. "Ember, are you controlling that thing?"

"I am, sir. You can talk with Mrs. Vintl. She'll confirm my ability with air magic." With a quick flick of their fingers, they released the air currents, letting the small twister dissipate. Ember wasn't sure they liked their parents lying to Mr. Elias, but they realized the growing number of people knowing their secrets had to stop.

Mr. Elias gave a self-mocking smile. "I'm sorry for the confusion. I guess when you study a topic for so long, you hope to meet the people you study, even if it isn't possible. As long as you're here, I guess I'll tell you Ember is doing well in class, despite some challenging students. They have a really good head on their shoulders."

Dad gave Mr. Elias his first genuine smile. "Thanks, we like to think so. I hope if you're right about those phoenixes that you do get to meet them some day."

It took an act of will to stop the groan and eye roll at that.

After a few more comments, the three of them left. Outside the room, they saw a flier for the Infinite WISDOM assembly the next day after school.

Dad stopped and stared. "Wisdom?"

Mom walked up and read the smaller print. "'*Witches In Superior Dominance Over Man.*' Idiots!"

Chapter 33 - The Blending of Magics

Daisy

Daisy sat in the backyard on a soft-cushioned pool chair. Her family didn't have a pool, but they did have a nice set of chairs and a table.

I bet my water magic would be better if I had a whole pool of water to practice with!

She'd placed two deep trays, one with water, one empty, on the table and sat back to contemplate what to do. The night before, she'd joked with her dad about water magic, and he'd challenged her to come up with a way to mix it with air magic. He didn't have air magic, so he didn't know what he was asking her to do.

Focusing on the water, she held her hand out, palm facing the water. She traced a path like an arch. The water took a similar but larger path from the full tray to the empty tray. A basic warm-up, as the teachers liked to say, to wake up her magic.

She made a small twister in one hand and tossed it to the other before releasing her air magic.

Okay, both water and air magic are 'warm,' so to speak.

A tree stood across the yard. Biting her lip, Daisy held her hands out, palms to the ground, then scooped them until they faced the clouds. Five water arrows rose from the water. Taking a breath, she thought about holding the arrows in her left hand. She flicked her right hand, focusing on the air currents, and the first arrow flew. It didn't hit the tree. The water fizzled out before reaching its target.

She tried again with a harder flick of the wrist. The second arrow flew apart over the yard, as did the third. With deep, slow breaths, she modulated how she manipulated the air, mimicking her mental control with how her right hand moved. The fourth arrow skimmed past the tree. But the fifth, the fifth splashed into the tree.

She slumped. *Do I want to do another set of arrows? Is that the only merging I can think of? Something violent? What else could I try?* She rubbed her temples, debating the ways she could mix her proficiencies.

After a few minutes of contemplating the issue, she sat up tall and held her hands apart, fingers curled in as if she held an invisible ball. Muscles tense, she pushed her power out, and the remaining water formed a sphere that sat in the tray on the table.

She licked her lips and tried to relax into the power that held the sphere in place. The first thing you learn in air magic is small twisters, thus the daily warm-ups. It's something kids who can do air magic play with. This should be easier than mixing water arrows and having them fly across the yard.

Daisy narrowed her eyes and created a small twister in the center of the sphere of water. It took concentration. The motion inside threatened to explode the water sphere apart. She immediately focused on keeping the sphere intact, securing the shape as the center spun. Once she felt she had the sphere contained, she allowed herself to watch the images and colors of the air in the water flashing out at her.

Her body started to tremble, but watching the beauty transfixed her. It was so worth it. She wished she'd set up the camera. She'd have to do that next time. It was amazing to see this. Ember would love it!

A chill ran down her back. She used more magic than she had in a long time, but she maintained the two spells, the patterns and colors playing across the edge of the sphere.

A buzzing in her pocket distracted her, and the swirling air broke through the globe as a shower of water exploded with the break in Daisy's concentration. She drooped as lank, wet hair dripped down her equally wet clothes. Digging out her phone, she answered without looking. "What?"

"Daisy? Is that you? Are you okay?"

Water dripped down Daisy's forehead. "Hi, Ember. Yeah, I'm fine." She tried to lighten her voice. "What about you?" Only half listening, Daisy put her phone on speaker and squeezed out her hair.

"I ... well ... there's something I need to talk to you about. It's, I don't want you to be mad, but I'm scared you'll be upset ... upset at me."

Hair and wet outfit forgotten, Daisy sat forward. "I'm sure you're overreacting. What could you do, save befriend one of the terrible three, that would make me upset with you?"

A soft chuckle came over the phone. *Is their voice lower than normal? Are they sick?* "It's definitely not that. Do you remember last weekend when you got upset that I had some secrets about fire?"

"Yeah, but part of it was that you had secrets, and part of it was that you told Felix before me. I hate to admit it, but I was jealous ... am jealous."

"Well, this isn't something Felix knows ... not really." Ember sounded hesitant, almost like they were distracted. After missing school on Monday and wearing a skirt today, Daisy couldn't be surprised with anything her friend said or did.

"Well, I'm glad you're telling me first. You know you can tell me anything, friend."

They laughed. "I know. Okay, here it is. Before I was born, Mom taught classes on air magic. She was a professor at a college."

"Oh my gods! Really? Does that mean she can tutor you?" Before Ember could answer, Daisy's mind caught up with what Ember had already said. "Wait, you don't need tutoring, do you? You've been holding back, haven't you?"

"I'm not going to anymore. I had this weird idea that I was blending in. I don't know where I got that idea, but, well, Mom's coming in tomorrow. We're going to do a demonstration on what the class is building towards. You know, with the platforms."

Excitement, frustration, happiness, anticipation, anger—so many emotions warred in Daisy. "So, you can already lift the platform? Is that what Mrs. Vintl called you back to class to discuss yesterday?"

There was a pause before Ember spoke. "Yeah. I floated mine to the ceiling, and she saw it. She convinced me my habit of hiding my magic was counterproductive."

Daisy snorted. "I could've told you that. I think I have told you that, like, almost every day."

"Yeah." They laughed. "I think you have too. I don't know what happened, except for a few stressful days. But, anyway, I really wanted to tell you about this before the big display at school. I don't want you to be surprised."

Daisy wanted to strangle Ember and hug them. Her best friend was finally embracing who they were, and more than even Daisy would finally know. All in all, she was proud of Ember and their willingness to finally embrace their abilities.

Ember can already fly that damn platform? It's really possible? Pride bubbled up through her gut at what her friend could do.

"Do you think your mom could give me some private lessons?"

Ember's warm voice came over the line, sounding more themselves. "Yes, of course."

Chapter 34 - Sometimes Being Brave Is Taking to the Skies

Ember

The beeping of Ember's alarm cut through their mind like a sledgehammer. They wanted nothing more than to curl under their covers and sleep the day away. They weren't sure why they'd agreed to the magical display with Mom in front of their class. When they'd presented the idea to Mom, it had been a fluke.

"Mom, why don't we show the class what flying on platforms is like? Lift up, toss the ball back and forth, and land? Maybe something small. Then Mrs. Vintl and the class will know what I can do, and they'll stop treating me like I'm magically stunted." A small laugh, and scene. That had been the plan. Simple and sweet.

What Ember hadn't counted on was theirt mom immediately grabbing onto the idea and running with it. She'd taken the phone number Ember had given for Mrs. Vintl, and scooted into the living room. "I'd like to meet with you on Thursday morning." Pause. "Yes, I know you have class." Pause. "If you bring the platforms outside, I can model one of the training exercises I used to do with Ember when they were young." Pause. "See you then."

Ember dropped into a chair in the kitchen, a boulder in their belly. "So, I'm not going to ease into this? Just a huge *bam!* of a display?"

"It'll be lovely, love," Mom said, then made some tea.

Walking to the air magic class, Ember and Daisy found a note on the door that class was being held in the South Field. Ember closed their eyes and sighed, resting their head on the door. *Right, Thursday ... it's happening today.*

Daisy chuckled and rubbed their back. "This will be amazing. You'll be amazing. Come on."

Behind them, a few others from class got to the door.

"Class is being held outside? What is that about?" Harry, one of the tenth year boys, asked.

Polly, another year ten who had lumbered up the stairs, replied, "No idea. Why couldn't they've told us this *before* we dragged ourselves and our bags up all these stairs?"

As they passed Simon, he turned and walked with them. "Is class canceled?"

"Mrs. Vintl is conducting class outdoors today," Daisy said as they reached the main hallway.

Simon started to turn the wrong way then spun to keep up with them. "What? But the ceiling in class opens. Why bother with outdoors?"

"Why bother with idiotic questions when we can all learn about the reason together?" Harry asked. "For someone so smart, you're sometimes kinda dumb, Simon. You know that, right?"

Simon rolled his eyes as they made their way to the South Field.

Once there, they found Mrs. Vintl and Ember's mom deep in discussion. The students saw two platforms, the green one Ember used in the class before and a black one, placed on the grass. Each one had a small basket with three balls attached to it. Ember smiled, remembering the setup from before they'd switched from homeschool to public.

Daisy clasped Ember's arm. "Are you really going to do this?" Her voice was low and full of awe.

Ember shrugged. "I guess."

Simon grabbed their arm. "What are you doing? What do you know?" In contrast to Daisy, he sounded accusatory, as if it were their fault he was losing a day of learning.

Before they could say more, Mrs. Vintl turned towards the students. "Good morning, everyone. Today, we're going to have a different type of class. On Tuesday, you learned that we want to advance our magic to lifting platforms. I asked you to imagine lifting yourself up and down, almost like an elevator. Today, I want to show you what you could do once you've mastered the skill."

Polly raised her hand. "Are you going to do something spectacular, Mrs. Vintl?"

The teacher blushed. "No, not me. I've invited someone who used to teach this class at a college level, someone whose skills are even better than my own."

Mom stepped up. "Hi, my name is Sadie Savita. I'm Ember's mom, and my specialty is air magic."

Simon guffawed. "If you're so good, why does Ember suck?"

Mom took a moment to stare at Simon blank-faced. Slowly, one of her eyebrows rose. Even if the intent of the question was fair, the way he asked it was beyond rude. Everyone looked back and forth between Simon and Mom until Simon blushed and mumbled, "Sorry."

With a bright smile, Mom replied, "That's an excellent question. My child doesn't, as you so eloquently put it, 'suck' at air magic. They never learned some of the basics, and when they started here, they decided to keep their skills hidden to ensure staying in the lower level classes. Well, that ends today. Ember and I will show you what you can do when you've really learned the element of air."

Everyone turned from Mom to Ember, and it took everything in Ember not to react.

Chapter 35 - Fire Bird, Air Bird

Ambrose

Ambrose sat in the sunroom, eating her prepared poached eggs, toast, and fruit salad. Her dad came out of the hall that led to his office and sat tall at the table. "Are you ready for this afternoon? Your presentation is very important. What starts in the secondary school extends to the parents, grows to the community, expands to the state, and then we've made it. It all starts with you and your friends."

"No pressure, Father." She barely stopped herself from rolling her eyes at him.

"I just want to make sure you're taking this seriously, Ambrose. You are so worried about your looks and that phone of yours. I just want you to be focused on this." His tone softened. "It's important, dear."

She gave him a tight smile and went back to eating. "I know. Mr. Shade's message is safe with me."

At school, Ambrose headed to class. She hadn't been able to talk to her teacher about losing her fire magic on Tuesday. She didn't like her father's answer. Class, as always, was held outside. Fire inside was a recipe for disaster.

She found Mr. Tine, the Fire Magic teacher, in the East Field, marking attendance on a clipboard of who walked up from the building. With a determined gait, Ambrose walked right up to him. "Mr. Tine, I need to talk to you, and it's important."

Still noting who was in attendance and not meeting her gaze, he made a small humming sound.

Why is he ignoring me? Doesn't he know I'm important? More important than most of the nobodies in this class.

Unwilling to be discouraged, she said, "During the class outing last weekend, there was a moment my fire magic evaporated for a few minutes. What could've caused that to happen?"

He made another mark in his notes. "Disappeared, right." His focus moved to the students coming from the school and back to his clipboard. Finally, he made eye contact with her, and his brow creased. "How do you mean? Can you explain the situation?"

She'd hoped he wouldn't ask this. "Well, there was some cloth I wanted to burn. The power was there, and suddenly it was gone. I just ... nothing." She threw her hands out to the side and shrugged. "I couldn't do anything with fire for several minutes."

Mr. Tine put the clipboard between his legs to hold it and rubbed his face with his hands. "The only time I've ever heard about someone losing their ability to use fire magic is when a more powerful user understood the proficiency to the point they could tamp another's flame."

Fear and awe overwhelmed Ambrose. "Can you do this?"

He grabbed the board and shook his head. "No. Not only is it something only a very powerful fire witch can do, it isn't my specialty. At the level we teach in this class, having that specialty doesn't matter, but at that level, it does."

She stepped away, thinking about that. Someone in the school, some eleventh year, had the ability to yank her fire away. It could've been one of the adults. *Actually, thinking about it, that makes more sense. If any of the students had the ability, they'd be in this class.* She searched the faces of her fellow students. *None of these nobodies would have the spine to do that to me. Worthless riffraff.*

"Welcome, class," Mr. Tine began. "I'm sorry we're starting a few minutes late, just getting a few administration things organized. Today, we're going to continue what we started on Tuesday. I would like you to create a—"

His mouth dropped open, and his eyes got wide. Everyone in class whipped around to follow his gaze. Ambrose's heart dropped to her bellybutton. Two platforms—one green, one black—were dancing in the air to her right. As she watched, a small ball flew from one towards the other. Then, it flew back, but it was low. The green platform dipped and darted to the side, and the rider, because there had to be a rider, must've gotten the ball.

Ambrose squinted, trying to see details. As the two platforms flew around the South Field, she realized the person on the black platform was some person, older, that she didn't know. *Is this just a demonstration? Nothing interesting, except as something I can't do?* Unable to stop watching, she decided she needed to determine who rode the green box of wood.

She licked her lips and took another step closer. At the distance they stood, the extra few steps didn't matter. When the rider flipped around, Ambrose gasped. Though far away, they were close enough for her to clearly see the rider had red hair. Only one student in this school had red hair: Ember.

Doubt and confusion were quickly chased by anger, then utter amusement. This person, this nobody of a student at their school who she and her friends had teased and mocked for years, now they decided to take to the skies in front of everyone? No, if Ember could always do this, they must have been mocking *them*. This was epically bad.

Turning her head, Ambrose realized every window in the school had a face staring out. Ember Savita had just gone from being the bratty human no one liked to an incredibly skilled magic practitioner that never admitted to anyone what they could do. Where she had to admit how hard hiding that level of ability would be, it irked her that there had been a secret she hadn't known.

She watched the display, a sneer twitching her upper lip. She began hating Ember for completely new reasons.

There was a new power in the school. And they were strong.

Chapter 36 - Where You Lead, They Will Follow

Ember

Ember trudged into the Magical History class. Playing catch with Mom was fun, thrilling even, but it'd been a while since they'd done that much concentrated magic, and Ember was exhausted.

They sat down and waited for class to start. There was to be a short lesson, followed by a quiz on the week's material. They were happy the amount of discussion would be curbed. They weren't sure they were up to whatever Ambrose and Cress would bring to the table today.

Felix sat down and swung to face Ember. "So, that was exciting."

"What was?"

"You do know that what you and your mom did was seen by, like, *everyone* in the school. You've gone from being a no-magic human wannabe to one of the most powerful practitioners in the class ... maybe the school, right? Literally, you will be the only thing talked about today. Maybe even tomorrow." He smirked.

Cold dread raced through their body. They opened their mouth then shut it. The visibility of the South Field didn't even occur to them when they set about to play catch.

Ambrose sauntered in, hips swishing. "If it isn't our resident magician. Poof, Ember Savita, going from a nobody to a somebody in one class period. Why, I think we should all stand and give them a round of applause, or would you rather we bow, your honor, the royalty of the air?" She rolled her eyes and dropped her bag. Her mocking tone had the effect of undoing any awe Ember and their mom had built up.

Students around the class who had been eyeing Ember, whispering, all laughed. Despite their laughter being ill-natured, at least it felt more natural then the awe they'd been faking a moment earlier. Though Ambrose had meant the comment to be mean, Ember was secretly happy to not be the center of so many conversations.

Ember leaned against their locker at the end of the day. The mixed reaction of the other students over the display of magic they'd done had taken its toll. All they wanted to do was leave. Felix stood in front of them and held their hands. "Do we really want to go to this thing? It'll probably make us stupider."

Ember laughed. "It absolutely will, but we promised Daisy."

"That we did, and she's our friend." He leaned down to touch his forehead to theirs. "It will also let us know what's going on in their camp, so we *should* go." He sighed. "Fine, we'll go."

"Yeah, that too. Information is power, or some such slogan."

Daisy came from down the hall. "Oh my gods! Are you two ready? This is going to be amazing. I know you're not fans of Ambrose or Cress, but someone must be their handler, giving them talking points, because last time they made *so* much sense! With practice, they'll convey the message even better. Like, epic, guys!"

Felix raised an eyebrow at her. "So, what you're telling us is you're excited?"

She slapped his arm. "Stop, not funny." She chuckled. "Should we go?"

"When does it start?" Ember asked.

"I think half past four."

"But it's not even four right now. What would we do?"

"Fine. Whatever, but fine." Daisy sounded annoyed, but her big smile told them she was jittery about the meeting.

They all tromped to the auditorium. Getting there early meant the choice of seats. Again, there was a large sign outside the doors explaining it was an event for Infinite WISDOM. In small letters under the acronym read *'Witches In Superior Dominance Over Man.'* There were pictures of Tad Shade, Mr. Wells – Ambrose's dad, Ambrose, and Cress. There were a few other pictures, but Ember didn't recognize them. A summary of what to expect took up the bottom of the sign in small print.

Felix shook his head. "They really aren't holding back with that acronym, are they? Putting it all out there, us or them."

Ember shot Daisy a quick glance, but she was ignoring them, already heading into the venue, off in her own world.

"You would think they'd wait until they had tapped more into the mob mentality to break out the crazy, but apparently they are confident," Ember agreed.

The three slipped in and sat in the back, much to Daisy's chagrin. "All the way back here? Why not up there?" She pointed to some seats near the front center.

Felix sighed. "I'd like to be able to see everything that's going down. If you don't mind. I mean, we'll be able to hear everything from back here too."

Daisy's face crumpled into a pout, something Ember didn't think was possible. She crossed her arms over her chest with a squawk. "Fine."

Ember noticed how many students there were that they'd thought were smarter than to fall for this claptrap, but then again, they were there.

Standing around the edge of the auditorium at regular intervals were several of the teachers and staff of the school. Some looked interested; some looked annoyed. *It's after school hours. I wonder if they volunteered or were told they had to come?*

Once all the seats were full, students sat on the steps between them.

Ember leaned closer to Felix. "That looks safe. Hope there isn't an emergency."

His mouth twitched into a smile. They noticed he'd placed his phone in a shirt pocket. Ember pointed to it and raised an eyebrow in question.

He gave them a full smile. "Recording it to share with my parents. They want to know what's going on. This is easier than trying to remember."

As he finished his explanation, Ambrose sauntered out, followed by Cress a few feet behind her. There wasn't a microphone this time. Squinting, Ember saw an earpiece with a thin wire pointing towards her mouth. "Friends, teachers, classmates." The wireless microphone reverberated well through the open space. "I am so glad you've chosen to join us today in your *infinite wisdom*. I am convinced that by the end of our presentation you will realize that our message is true and that we have nothing but positive messages to share."

She held out her arms to the side with a soft smile, waiting for the jubilant applause to abate. "Though witches and humans have different schools and many of you have grown up separated from humans, once you get into the working world, our jobs are often integrated. You can talk with your parents and learn the truth about the equality between magic users and humans and the fallacy of that story. After the war, humans were scared, and equality was in their best interest, but because of the laws put in place, they became emboldened, and over the years, they've decided we are weak, unworthy, and beneath them."

On the other edge of the audience, a boy from air magic class, Harry Lows, stood up. "Where is the evidence of these opinions? I've worked with humans as a volunteer in a lab for three years, and not once have I heard an inkling of any of this."

Cress stiffened, expression hard. He narrowed his eyes at Harry and snapped, "If you reviewed the links on the back of our flier from last week, you would know."

"I *did* review the *one* link. It just went to your shell of a website. There wasn't anything but base propaganda explaining why your group was great. No evidence about what you were claiming. So again, where is the evidence? Will we get it this week?"

Ambrose placed a placating hand on Cress's arm and smiled wide at Harry. "Of course, you did, and we're very thankful that you were so diligent." Her hand slid up to her ear, and her voice lowered. "Josie, fix this before the end of the meeting." Ember was pretty sure no one was supposed to hear that.

Cress stepped forward. "Both Ambrose and I have easily found the evidence. The bookstore off Main which denied entry to a group of students from our school last year. A coffee shop that only serves witches after nine in the morning to ensure no human is late to work. I'm surprised someone as clever as you, Harry, working in a lab, couldn't find the links on your own with a few keystrokes yourself. A simple search. The humans are very much in agreement that they are superior to us in our diminished numbers and should lead us to oblivion."

Ember wondered about these stories. Cress didn't give the names of the establishments, just vague generalities. It would be enough for a lot of the students to believe. They saw Harry across the room roll his eyes and shake his head as he sat. They felt much the same.

Tansy stood. "Are our numbers diminished? Spots in secondary schools are harder and harder to get. That would lead one to think the number of teens is *increasing,* not *decreasing.* Are there studies showing the population of magic users on your flier as well?" She sat as she finished her question.

Taking a deep breath, Ambrose forced a smile. "These questions are, of course, excellent. Yes, we'll make sure all the links you need are on our website. It's new, and our staff didn't know how smart our audience would be. We tried to warn them, but they just hear 'teens.' You know, adults." She waited for the laughter to abate. "We will make sure all your needs are met." She shimmied with a wide eyed smile. "Now, if you could hold all questions until the end, thank you. Back to our presentation. The humans would like to utilize our abilities but not allow the magic users any position of political power. Up until now, the two groups have led in *representational* equality."

Cress stepped forward. "In other words, because there are so many more humans, we have very few of our people within the hallowed halls of the government. We've never had a witch president, only a few representatives, and fewer judges. Because of this, the humans already control us, but is that enough?"

He waited for the crowd to yell 'no.' He seemed to instinctively know what to do. Cress gave them a winning smile. "Of course not. They want more. They don't want us anywhere near making or controlling the laws. They think we have too much power being able to control the elements. We have our proficiencies, and that is too much for them. If they had their way, they'd make us their workers, their slaves, or, in the best case scenario, ejected from their nation all together. As if *that* were possible."

The students in the crowd went wild, stomping their feet and making noise.

Ember sat mute. The two popular kids drove their point home, regardless of the hecklers in the audience. It was awful. They manipulated the thoughts and fears, and the majority of the students followed happily. Gazing around the room, they noticed several of the teachers nodded slowly as well.

Up on the stage, a glow of elation seemed to infuse Ambrose as the students cheered. Sliding their focus to Felix, Ember saw the same look of disgust on his face. His normal poker face was gone. To their left, Ember saw Daisy leaning forward, her face the wide-eyed wonder of someone who'd heard something that changed their view of life.

Daisy's hand reached out and tightened on Ember's arm. "This is fantastic, don't you think?"
Ember felt nauseous.

Chapter 37 - Have Your People Call My People

Ember

Ember sat at the kitchen table, eating a bowl of oatmeal for breakfast. They'd added nuts and craisins and had a huge mug of coffee. Dad joined them with his own coffee, a bagel with cream cheese and jam, and a hard-boiled egg. "Will that be enough, Ember? I could peel an egg for you."

"Sure, yeah, maybe."

"Wow, you sound ready for school."

Ember put down their spoon. "Yesterday started with the magic display—no more questions about whether or not I can do magic—and ended with that damn circus run by Ambrose and Cress. They're going to be more popular than ever after that. Everyone fawning over them."

"Are you jealous of the attention?" He waggled his brows with a grin.

"What? Gods, no! Gross. They're just going to be more impossible. Their message spouted by more people. And then there's the fact that it's going to get worse. Look at this." Ember tossed the flier from Thursday's event. It announced the next big rally would be a city-wide one the following Saturday, just over a week away. There would be a list of presenters, including the school's very own Ambrose and Cress. Ember could puke.

He sipped his coffee. "Anything that would make you feel better?"

"A flight. It's been too long. I need time in the clouds." The idea of the peace of the skies made them itch for it even more.

A smile crinkled his face. "What, zooming in the air in front of your classmates with Mom wasn't enough?" They glared at him, and he chuckled. "Got it. Okay, a flight sounds lovely, my dear. How about tomorrow? You, me, Mom. We'll drive out to the woods north of here. We need to check in with Roan and crew anyway—it's been too long. Check the wards. Our land's protections need their regular updates."

After taking a sip of coffee, Ember gazed into the dark depths. "Can Felix come with?"

Dad nearly dropped his mug of coffee. "What? Really?"

They shrugged. "Why not? He knows our secret. I bet he'd love it."

"Mom and I will discuss. Now, finish up. You'll be late."

Ember met Felix and Daisy in study hall. They sat at the back of the room with their books out. There was a big exam in Spanish class they needed to study for.

They started quizzing each other, trying to help prepare for the class.

About halfway through class, Olivia came in ... late. Olivia was never late. She stood in the door, gazed around, then came over to sit with the three of them. Her eyes were red-rimmed, as if she'd been crying, and her face was pale.

Ember smiled. "Hi, Olivia. You okay?"

She bit her lip and shook her head. "Sorry for interrupting you, I just ... I didn't know who I could talk to, and you're always so nice."

"Of course, you can sit with us. What's wrong?"

Her head darted back and forth, checking out the other students in the classroom. She leaned in and spoke low. "Did you go to that ... farce yesterday?"

Daisy's brows came together, and she was about to say something when Ember put a hand on her arm. "We were there. Why?"

"You know how Tansy, well, Tansy and Harry spoke up, asked questions?"

Daisy's nose scrunched up. "They interrupted."

Olivia didn't seem to hear or see Daisy's disapproval. "Right. Anyway, Tansy's mom called me last night. Tansy got beat up after school. No one knows who did it because she hasn't woken up. The doctors think ... hope ... she'll wake up today. Harry's there too. They were both admitted." She sniffled, and a tear ran down her face. "They live in different directions, went home using different routes, but they ended up in the same emergency room. Gods above, who would've done that to her ... to them?"

Daisy, eyes wide and misty, gasped. "They're both in the hospital? That's awful."

A cold fist of dread punched into Ember's chest. They moved over and hugged Olivia. She squeezed Ember back. Their eyes slanted to Felix, whose face had gone hard.

Ember slid back into their seat and saw Daisy. Their friend looked to be both shocked and trying to puzzle it all out.

Ember attempted to calm themself as anger replaced their shock. They slid an arm around Olivia. "That's awful. I'm so sorry. I'll ... maybe I can go and check on her tomorrow. I'm going a bit north with my family tomorrow morning, but maybe in the afternoon."

Olivia tried to smile. "That would be good ... if she wakes up. She's in room 416B. Call ahead. Make sure she's taking visitors. She likes you."

Ember smiled. "I like her too."

The four spent a few minutes staring at their books. Ember doubted any of them were really focused enough to study. Finally, Felix turned to look at them. "You're going up north tomorrow?"

Ember gave him a genuine smile, a lightness blossoming in them. "I talked to Dad about it this morning. If Mom agrees, I was going to invite you ... if you're free. An escape for a few hours."

Out of the corner of their eye, Ember saw Daisy's face harden. They should've waited to invite Felix when she wasn't around. There was just so much going on with people in the hospital and the air show and the obnoxious assembly. Ember debated saying something to Daisy, though they didn't know what.

Felix smiled, tilting his head and giving them a quirky half shrug. "My schedule *is* pretty busy, but I may be able to carve some time out for you. Have your people call mine, and we'll let you know."

Ember snorted and finally focused enough to get back to studying.

Chapter 38 - If You Don't Mind, Look over There

Ember

Saturday morning, the day was perfect. The sky shone a gorgeous cerulean blue, speckled with a few clouds. The temperature was lovely, not that it would matter. Once Ember shifted into their bird form, the temperature became moot. They drove with their parents and Felix along the coast, north, to a wooded area seldom seen by people.

Felix watched as they drove. "I've never heard of North Droster Woods. Does it have walking trails?"

Mom chuckled. "Yes and no. It's on private property owned by our family. No one comes to these woods who isn't invited. There are wards in place. We're going to have to introduce you to the protections so that you're safe during your visit."

Felix's eyes widened. "Am I in any danger?"

"Aren't you always?" Dad joked.

They passed a road, and the woods began. A wrought iron fence, at least ten feet tall, separated the road from the trees. As they drove, Felix kept looking in the other direction. "So, how long until we get there?"

Ember pointed out the window that faced the property, but Felix barely shifted his focus before shrugging. "Is it very long?"

Ember gazed at Felix and thought back to when they were five or six.

Their mom was speaking to them. "Ember, love, these woods belong to our family—me, your dad, and now you."

"It's so much land, and it's all ours?"

"It sure is, dear," Dad said. "And we've put protections up."

"What kind of protection?"

"Just know that me or Mom need to be here the first time anyone comes. There is magic Mom and some friends put around the land in the fence. It makes the place invisible so we can fly in peace."

Ember smiled wide at their parents. "The land is magical?"

They shook their head. "Mom?" Ember asked. "What exactly am I missing?"

"Ten minutes, dear." She shot Ember a look before shaking her head then turning back to the road. "We'll be there, and Dad and I will explain everything."

The car pulled up to the gate. The fence stretched in both directions as far as a person could see. The gate itself was as wide and tall as a large truck, stylized with vines and flowers. There was a number pad with privacy sides attached to the gate that allowed for entry. Dad reached out. His hand slid into the box, and a moment later, the gate quietly opened.

Throughout the process, Felix had his eyes closed and rubbed his forehead. Concerned but realizing there was nothing they could do, Ember rubbed his back.

A small moan escaped him as they drove past the gate, and then his head snapped up as he shivered. "What just happened?"

Dad stopped the car. "Everyone out. We'll explain in a moment."

Everyone piled out. Mom put her hand on the gate, and it flared a royal blue. Then everyone got back into the car, and they continued to drive.

Mom turned. "There are wards on the fence and gate. They not only keep people out, there is a level of mind magic built in, a 'don't see me' message. I can do a bit of manipulation, but I have to touch the gate to add or subtract people. If we come again, it won't be as painful for you."

Felix nodded. "It has been a long time since anyone has gotten the drop on me with mind magic. That must be very powerful."

"It is. And old. With age it gets stronger."

It took several more minutes to get to a clearing. Again, everyone piled out. Dad moved to the back of the truck, pulling out camp chairs and a cooler. Mom looked up to the top of the tall trees and whistled. Happiness bubbled in Ember as they looked up to the sky. They loved the sentries that protected the land. "Do you think they'll fly with us today?"

Dad chuckled. "Probably not, dear. They have a job to do here."

Felix mimicked them, head thrown back. "What are we looking for?" He turned in place searching for ... something.

Ember smiled, excitement bubbling in them. "Our security, so they can meet you. Once that's done, Dad and I can get in the air and fly. Gods, it's been too long."

A rustling sound came to them. A few seconds later, three griffons flew down to land surrounding them. They were taller than any of them with bodies of red-furred lions, heads of eagles, and large, powerful snow-white wings.

Felix's head dropped with the majestic beasts, and once they landed, he landed on his butt. His eyes grew to the size of saucers, and his mouth had dropped open. "How?"

Ember ran up to the middle one. "Zorn! It's been too long. Have you been keeping yourself safe?" They wrapped their arms around the beast's neck.

Zorn shook its head and made a sniffling sound.

Turning to the beast to Zorn's left, Ember scratched its neck. "Tort, are you keeping these two in line? It's a hard job, but someone has to do it." The beast bent its front legs and bowed.

Ember moved to the third. "Roan, as leader of this crew, I'd like you to meet my friend, Felix. He is considered safe and a friend." Ember led Roan over to Felix, who sat like a statue as the beast sniffed him. "Thank you for the protection of you and your brothers." Ember bowed their head, and Roan tipped its back.

The three griffins turned to look at Ember's mom. She smiled and signaled, and the three leapt to the air.

Once out of sight, Felix gulped in some air. "They're real?"

"Of course, dear. Didn't anyone tell you about magical creatures and shapeshifters?" Mom stared at him in teacher mode.

"Yes, but, no, but, wait, are they shapeshifters?" Felix sounded awed.

"Not those three. There are some griffin shifters that live up in Alaska, but they have stayed in their own community for years. I doubt you'll ever meet them," Dad said, coming up behind Felix. "Ember, I think it's time. If you want to get in a good flight, maybe go out over the ocean, we'd better get out there now."

As they turned to the car, Ember heard Felix say quietly, "Okay."

Giddy with the thought of finally shifting, Ember followed their dad behind the car. They might be dating Felix, but shifting where he could watch was a bit more intimate than they were ready for. The shift was relatively quick, and once they were phoenixes, they both stretched their wings and flew.

Chapter 39 - A Dream Come True

Felix

Ember and their dad headed behind the car to change. Their mom pointed to the camp chairs. "Let's set these up. We can watch them and talk. There are some sodas and water in the cooler if you get thirsty."

He helped her set up the four camp chairs and a fold-up table. Sitting, he searched for the three griffins. *How the hell did creatures that big hide? They were amazing ... and real.*

"How long does it take Ember and their dad to shift?"

A bird flew up from behind the car. No ... a phoenix! It was huge, the size of a large dog. Its white back feathers shimmered in the sun with orange and red wings. As it lifted into the air, Felix saw that its belly was an iridescent blue. The tail feathers flowed down a few feet as it cleared the top of the trees, a mix of the white, orange, and red feathers. Once the phoenix reached its desired height, it stretched out its wings and circled the small clearing.

Felix's heart nearly stopped in his chest, and he realized his mouth hung open.

"About that long, dear. Maybe three to five minutes. It depends on how they feel and how long it's been. Just wait. Ember is prettier, if you ask me. I just love their phoenix colors."

Excitement almost stopped Felix's ability to think. He'd dreamed of this day, seeing phoenixes in real life, and never thought it would happen. Everyone knew they were extinct, yet here he was, seeing one in the air above his head. Ember's dad in bird form was majestic. He couldn't imagine what 'prettier' could even mean.

Ember leapt into the air from behind the car, a blaze of fire. Their phoenix feathers burned a deep red all over their body. Their tail trailed down in a waterfall of red, orange, and purple. Once they reached the height of their dad, their wings snapped out, and Felix realized the deep-red of their body faded to orange and then to a deep purple. They were breathtaking.

The two raced around then disappeared in the direction of the ocean. Felix's heart pounded with his excitement. As the phoenixes disappeared, he sipped his soda, and his brain seemed to finally start to work. "That was ... oh my gods. I can't ... wow."

"I know. I was awe struck the first time I saw Ash and his twin take to the skies all those years ago." Ember's mom's voice helped to ground Felix.

He shook his head and took a deep breath. "So, have you thought about my parents' offer for you all to come to the meeting tomorrow?"

Despite talking to Ember's mom, Felix refused to take his eyes off the sky. He wouldn't miss the two returning.

"We've discussed it, and we don't know if we're ready. I know that you and your parents think this organization is the right fit for us, but we've spent a lot of years protecting us and our family. We don't want to endanger Ember."

"Has Ember shared with you what's been going on in the assemblies at school?"

Mrs. Savita sighed. "Yes. It's awful. The habit of people to listen and follow without hearing the words is ridiculous. It's an epidemic when the hordes stop thinking for themselves. I can't believe this group wants to dismantle two hundred years of peace in this country, and for what? A bit of power? Having this power over the non-magic-users won't help within the magical world. It will only harm the others. It's all just awful."

The two phoenixes returned, trailing fire in their wakes. Felix realized their tails were on fire. They began flying in a tight pattern, creating abstract fire art in the sky above them. Watching them, the fire, the white streak, the red streak ... Felix realized he'd stopped breathing. His mouth hung open again as the two streaked above him. Then, as quickly as they came in, they were gone, back towards the sea.

Once the afterimages of their antics had dissipated, he shook his head and shut his mouth. It took a second to recall what Mrs. Savita had last said to him. "You're right. If no one works against Tad Shade and his army, they will work to have humans downgraded to peasants or slaves. Everything I've seen or heard is ignorant and disgusting, and the worst thing is, people are eating it up. It's like magic users are forgetting that they *know* humans, *work with* humans, *have friends* that are human, and suddenly, all humans are just the enemy. Common sense has left the building. I don't understand how so many people can be so blinded to the truth."

In his peripheral vision, Felix saw Mrs. Savita rub her face. "Mob mentality. It's easy to follow the crowd, give up your need to make a decision, and just flow with the actions of those around you. It's how all the worst parts of history have happened."

"Yeah, I guess. I just can't imagine not thinking and realizing how awful those actions are."

She placed a hand on his arm. "I know, dear. You're one of the good ones."

Ember flew back into the sky, then slowly descended until they hovered right in front of them, their majestic body filling Felix's full vision. Suddenly, to the side, in fire, were the words, '*How long?*'

Mrs. Savita's face scrunched up. "How long until what, hon?"

'*Until you need us back.*'

"I'll call."

Ember extended their wings then pulled them in, spiraling their body straight up into the sky. Specks rained from their body. Once at altitude, they darted away.

"Did ... words ... fire ... appear ... communicate ... what?" Felix worried about his brain melting after the number of shocks it had received today.

"Yes, phoenixes have spectacular skill with fire. Ember can create words, sentences even, with their fire. It's how we can communicate when they're in bird form."

He watched the space where the words had been as the afterimage of the letters burned in his vision. Mouth dry, he sipped his soda. A smile slowly spread on his face. "I can't believe this is happening. This is so amazing. Like, phoenixes, real phoenixes, flying around the woods, and I get to see them, and talk to them."

"And date one, dear."

He laughed then realized it sounded a bit maniacal. "And date one. Gods above, that's unreal. This is like a dream. All my life, I've studied them, and a week ago, they became real. Ember became real, and now this. I just ..." Lost for words, he just watched the sky above.

"I know, dear ... I know."

"What were those sparkles that fell from Ember as they spiraled up?"

Mrs. Savita smiled. "Ember used a bit of air magic to propel themselves up. They like combining different proficiencies, and flying while manipulating air currents allows for some extra fun. When they use witch magic in bird form, they rain sparkles."

His jaw dropped again. He really did worry about his brain exploding, or melting, or its overall integrity for the day.

They sat watching the skies in companionable silence for several minutes, drinking soda and enjoying the day.

Fire letters erupted in front of them, each word fully formed as if being spoken. '*The beach is full of humans. No ocean antics today.*'

Mrs. Savita shut her eyes and drooped. "That beach is part of our land. There are signs and warnings. We're going to have to reset our wards and talk to local authorities about this. I know we aren't out here often, but when we *do* come here, it would be nice for those two to be able to fly where they want to fly. That was the point of purchasing this area."

"Will this end their flight?"

"Not end it." She searched the woods as if looking for something. "But limit them to land. They can fly fast, and over the ocean gives them a freedom to really move. Though these woods are big, they aren't *that* big."

"Why can't they fly over the ocean?"

A look of frustration crossed Mrs. Savita's face. "With their speed, they can create waves or trails in the water. It's a risk not worth taking with a full beach."

"Do you think any of the people on the beach saw them?" Fear gripped him.

"No, dear." The certainty in her words let him relax back in his seat. "Phoenixes have their own type of magic to avoid detection."

About twenty to thirty minutes later, two fireballs hurtled through the skies above. Right above them, the phoenixes snapped out their wings to hover, flames licking from the edges of their wings, their tails swishing. They started to descend, the fire in their wings dissipating.

"Felix wanted to know if the people on the beach could've seen you. Can you alleviate his fears?" Mrs. Savita asked with a laugh in her voice.

In a blink, they both disappeared. They were just gone. He shook his head and wondered if he'd imagined the whole day. Doubt plagued him. He rubbed his eyes and realized there was no way he could've spent the day watching phoenixes. That was crazy. They'd died out centuries ago. This was all just a fun joke Ember's family had played on him. They were such a playful family.

They reappeared, and his head started to pound. Mrs. Savita handed him a bottle of water. "Your head will be fine in a couple of minutes. Just relax."

"That was more than disappearing, wasn't it."

She nodded slowly. "Its invisibility coupled with doubt and confusion. It wiggles through the mind, erasing all memories and confidence in having seen a phoenix. We've tested it with some of the strongest mind mages we know, and nothing can counter it. It's one of the reasons we can stay hidden, even though over the years Ash needed to fly and now Ember does as well."

Felix just blinked and drank his water. "And all of this is confidential, right?"

"Yes. If people knew these secrets, the power wouldn't be as effective. You can tell your parents—we discussed this when Ember asked if you could join us today—but we ask that the information stop with you and them."

"Okay, yeah. That makes sense. I may not tell them everything I learned. They don't need to know most of it. What I do share, they can keep secret as well as I can."

Ember walked from around the car, dressed and smiling. "I really needed that. The full beach, not so much, but everything else. It has been way too long."

Felix stood and gave them a hug. "You are amazing ... in both forms, in *any* form."

They laughed. "I'm glad I don't have to keep secrets. It's freeing. Keeping it from Daisy is a necessity, but having someone besides my parents ... it's nice."

As happy as the words made Felix, a sense of sadness filled him as well. He knew Daisy was like a sister to Ember, and not being able to trust her with this would be hard.

They sat down in the camp chairs, and Felix heard Ember's belly grumble. They groaned. "So hungry."

Mrs. Savita handed them two sandwiches, a bag of chips, and a soda. "This should tide you over until lunch."

Chapter 40 - Either You're with Us or You're Against Us

Ember

Ember and their Dad ate. Flying took a lot of energy, and they could feel their muscles shake as they finished their first ham and cheese sandwich and started in on their second. They'd wanted to play a bit more, flying over the ocean, but all those people ruined it.

"Once you've finished, we can head back into town. Do we need to do anything before we go home?" Mom said. "Felix, did you want a sandwich, chips?"

"Sure, sounds great." She handed him one of each.

"I'd like to stop at the hospital, but I should call first," Ember said.

Dad tilted his head at them in question.

They explained about Tansy and Harry asking questions at the rally and not making it to school on Friday. "I just want to check up on them. Tansy's a friend ... sort of. I like her. She stands up to Josie—she has spunk. I don't know Harry as well, but he *is* in my air magic class."

Mom looked worried. "Well, you know where the cell service picks up better than we do. We can either all go to the hospital, or we can drop you at home and one of you can drive. It isn't far."

In the end, Felix drove Ember to the hospital. It was the one that specialized in magical treatments. Tansy was awake, but visiting hours didn't start for a couple of hours. They got home, had a second lunch like proper hobbits, and then headed out.

When they got to the hospital, Ember walked up to the information desk to check in. "Hi, we're here to see Tansy Styrke. She's in room 416B."

The woman behind the desk started typing on her computer. "Names."

"Ember Savita and Felix Porter."

"Friends or family?"

Ember bit their lip. They thought the answer was obvious but didn't want to push the lady. She could deny them access. "Friends."

"Down the hall. Follow the purple tiles, go through the atrium, take elevator 'H.' Go up to the fourth floor. It's simple from there, but you can check in with the nurses station and ask for directions if you need them."

Once she was done giving her directions, she handed them each an orange sticker that said 'visitor,' then turned away, their presence dismissed.

Ember put the sticker on their chest and followed the purple line on the floor. There were also signs that stated the direction to elevator 'H.' Despite the size of the building, it was well marked.

The Atrium took up as much room as the food court in the mall. In the center stood a coffee station that Felix dragged Ember to. They waited in line. Ember gazed up at the windowed ceiling. "I would hate to be the person who had to clean those. I mean, I love heights and the outdoors, but that would just suck." As they watched, a few birds landed on one of the windows.

He snorted. "I agree, but the windows and wood and sculpted iron-patterned ceiling is stunning."

They continued to watch the sky and clouds as they made their way to the front of the line.

"Three coffees with milk and sugar."

Snapped out of the clouds, Ember watched as Felix paid. "Three? Do you think they'll let Tansy have a coffee? And how do you know how she drinks it?"

"If they won't, I'll drink a second one. After your family muddled my brain, I need something to put it to rights."

Ember laughed, and they continued their trek along the Purple Brick Road. They soon came to a field of poppies, or a hexagonal area with a couple of restrooms and several banks of elevators. Finding the ones topped with the 'H,' Ember pressed the up arrow. As they waited, a few people in scrubs joined them, also holding steaming mugs that Ember assumed were coffee.

When the elevator doors opened, they all piled in. Various floor numbers were selected, including the button for the fourth floor, not by Ember or Felix. When they finally arrived, they disembarked with one of the people in scrubs. There were two hallways. They chose the one marked '*B-wing.*' Just past the nurses' station, they saw a sign with room numbers and arrows. Navigation continued to be quick and easy.

Tansy's room was the fifth room on the right. When they got there, she was alone. Ember knocked.

Tansy's voice came to them, thin and wispy. "Hi, Ember. Come in. It's nice to see you."

"I have Felix with me."

"Even better. There are two chairs in here. It's nice to have visitors." Ember and Felix went and sat as Tansy continued to speak. "They said I should be able to go home tomorrow if I can walk without too much pain."

Tansy lay in the hospital bed in a light-blue gown with tiny faded flowers on it. A pale-yellow blanket draped over her. Ember could just see a bandage around her body and a cast on her arm.

Felix handed her a coffee, and her eyes lit up. "Oh gods, thank you. They gave me a small cup in the morning, but I can't seem to convince them to give me more." She took a sip and moaned. "Oh gods, cream and sugar. You're angels, aren't you, just pretending to be fellow students and friends?"

Ember laughed with Tansy, and then Tansy coughed, her face scrunching up and her eyes closing and watering with the pain.

"What happened to you?" Ember asked quietly, afraid of the world opening up to them now. They knew this had to do with the assembly and Tansy speaking up and questioning Ambrose. The idea that asking questions could land someone here ... a chill went down their spine.

"I don't know a lot. I was walking home, and three guys came at me from different directions. They were big, thick, old—maybe in their twenties or thirties. I couldn't really tell. I tried to cross the street, but they blocked me."

Felix leaned forward. "You were alone? You didn't recognize them?"

"I have no idea who they were. One yelled at me, 'Are you a human lover?' The second shouted, 'Look at the human sympathizer!' The third, he just started kicking and punching. I managed to hit the emergency signal on my phone before I lost consciousness. When I woke up, it was today. Two days after the attack, I still had three broken ribs, two broken arms, and a concussion. But, in the end, I'm alive and on some very good drugs."

Felix's face morphed into a mask of fury. "Do you still have broken bones? Didn't they bring in a medical specialist? Your bones should be set and healed. It's been two days."

Tansy bit her lip. "They did, several times. Two of my ribs and my right arm are healed. Apparently, they can only fix so many broken bones at a time. The body goes into shock. They'll do another round this evening or tomorrow morning, depending on how my body is doing. By late tomorrow morning, I should be all fixed, *and again,* if I can walk, I can go home."

A nurse walked in with a lanyard around her neck with the hospital's name on it. Her name tag was backwards, but Ember assumed it would be her name and picture. On the lanyard was a tiny infinity sign hidden amongst her other personal buttons. For a moment, they wondered if it had to do with math, science, or something else.

She gazed at each of them, then gave a winning smile to Felix. "I hate to throw you out, but we need to get our patient prepared for her next round with the healer. The process of mending bones takes a few hours. You could possibly call and visit tomorrow." With her message delivered, she turned her back to them and began her medical measurements on Tansy.

Ember quietly snorted at the treatment. "Hopefully we'll see you soon, Tansy."

"Bye, you two."

Before they left, Ember dragged Felix to the information desk. The same woman sat, still apparently unhappy to see them. "I was wondering if Harry Lows was available for visitors."

The woman sighed. "You two just want to visit everyone today, don't you?" Her fingers clacked on the keyboard as she watched her monitor with a bored expression. Suddenly she sat up tall and leaned in, moving the mouse and pounding the button with her finger. She went back to typing, periodically shooting Ember a quick glance. Finally, she sighed and sat back. "I'm sorry. Harry Lows is no longer admitted as a patient here."

Ember wanted to feel happy, but something about this woman's demeanor told them that 'happy' wasn't the right emotion. "So, he checked out? Is he back home?"

The help-desk woman rubbed her eyes. "No, I'm sorry. He didn't make it. I really don't know any more details. Again, I'm really very sorry."

A cold chill ran down Ember's spine. Harry had died.

Chapter 41 - A Friend in Need Is a Friend Believed

Ember

Tansy was released from the hospital Sunday morning. Ember called and arranged for a few of them to meet at her house for lunch to make sure she was really doing better. When Ember called Daisy, they were happy to hear she wanted to join in.

Felix drove, and when they arrived, they found Olivia there. They sat in a well-appointed living room. A large black leather couch took up space across from the picture window. Tansy lay curled at one end of the couch, a blanket tucked in around her. A table at the end of the couch held a steaming cup of something ... coffee? Tea? On the other end of the couch, Olivia sat. The two were smiling and talking.

Perpendicular to the couch was a matching love seat. It also had small tables at each end. Ember and Felix sat on the smaller couch. Facing the love seat was a recliner chair. Daisy claimed it and immediately popped out the footrest.

Tansy's mom smiled at them. "Coffee? Tea?"

"I'll take a coffee with sugar and cream," Felix said with a smile.

Ember nodded. "Sounds perfect."

Daisy bit her lip. "I'll have whatever is easiest for you, but tea would be lovely."

She smiled and headed away.

"Did you hear about Harry? One of the nurses told me, but I haven't seen or heard anything from the school," Tansy said, her eyes down, and she wrung her hands.

Ember nodded. "I asked if we could visit him after you. They told me but not really any details."

Daisy's eyebrows came together. "Wait, what did I miss?"

"Oh, I thought I told you; in all the hustle and bustle of yesterday, it must've gotten lost." Ember bit their lip.

"He didn't survive his injuries." Daisy's eyes widened. "Look, I'm really sorry. I thought you knew."

"Can we start at the beginning?" Daisy had lost all her color. "What exactly happened? How did the two of you end up in the hospital in the first place?"

Before Tansy could answer, Felix sighed. "I don't know that you want to hear all of this, Daisy. It has to do with the assembly and the people who disagree with the message being given."

Her face hardened, not a common look for Daisy. "That just can't be true."

Tansy shifted to better face Daisy. "But it is. When they attacked me, they referenced my question from the assembly. If I hadn't asked my question, I wouldn't have had five broken bones, a concussion, and so many days in the hospital."

Daisy's eyes looked a bit crazy, and she leaned forward. Her muscles tensed as if she were ready to fight.

Ember knew that wasn't going to help anyone. They rubbed their eyes. "Okay, we came here to celebrate Tansy's health and send our best wishes up to Harry, who I think we all knew in one way or another. If we can light a candle, we can each write a goodbye to him and burn it, sending it up to him. Then, we can shift our focus and move on to the living."

There was a moment of silence as everyone adjusted from the fight they'd been denied to thinking about Harry. Tansy's mom returned with two coffees and a tea.

"Mom," Tansy asked. "Do we have a candle we can use to burn some paper?"

Her mom's brow furrowed. "Why not go out to the fire pit? I'll even bring you some marshmallows, chocolate bars, and graham crackers. Nothing like s'mores after remembering a friend who's passed."

"Thanks, Mom!"

They headed to the backyard, and Ember and Felix began building up the wood for a fire. Once they were done, Tansy's mom said, "Let me find a match. I know there's one around here."

Olivia said, "Don't worry. I've got it." She waved her hand, and a respectable fire erupted from the center of the firepit.

Tansy asked her for paper and pens, and once they were set, they each spent a few minutes thinking about Harry.

Harry, I'm sorry I didn't get to know you better. You were funny in air magic class, and I was impressed with how you stood up for yourself during that assembly. I wish it hadn't led to your getting hurt. I will try to fight the good fight that you started with that question. ~Ember

Once everyone finished writing a note to Harry, they each burned their words in the heat of the flames.

Afterwards, they told stories about Harry and their memories of him in class. Then, they found sticks and roasted marshmallows. After the first one, Felix said he had an appointment, and the three headed out.

As they arrived at Daisy's house, before she got out of the car, she mumbled, "I can't believe they think it was Infinite WISDOM that put them in the hospital. That's crazy. The group is good. They want to help magic users, not harm them. Tansy is just wrong."

Chapter 42 - We Will Fight the Good Fight!

Felix

"Don't worry about Daisy. She'll come to her senses." He could tell Ember was hurt by the way they slumped in the seat and the drawn look in their eyes. Their best friend was blindly following this new movement.

Three years ago when Ember came to our school, they were lost and alone. Daisy was the only one who was nice to them, made them feel welcome. They've been inseparable ever since, siblings of the heart. And now Ember's heart is breaking as Daisy is taken by this group that me and my parents have been working against for so long.

He parked outside their house. "My parents and I are heading to a meeting for the FB Coalition. I was really hoping you and your family would be joining us."

"I know, and maybe in the future. For right now, they want to continue to gather information." They still sounded distracted, but Felix held out hope.

"What about you?"

"Maybe next week. I've had too much 'new' this week. I just want to lie down and decompress. After the field trip last weekend, and all of the crazy that happened this week, I think I just want to have a few hours of nothing." They'd been staring at their hands but slowly looked up into Felix's eyes. "Is that okay?"

He reached over and cupped their face. Leaning in, he kissed them. "Of course. Next weekend would be perfect."

Ember got out of the car, and he watched as they disappeared into their house. Once the door shut, he headed home.

I know things are hard for Ember and their family, but having them join us would be amazing. Even if they couldn't and wouldn't share who they are, their history and knowledge alone would add so much to what we're trying to do. I hope we can get them involved. We really need them.

His mom and dad waited in the living room. They stood when he entered. Mom said, "Do you need to do anything to get ready? We have someone we're meeting at the FB gathering. We don't want to be late."

"You convinced Ember's parents?"

"No, dear, someone else. We'd love to have the Savitas join us, but we'll have to wait for them to agree. Your history teacher, Mr. Elias. We ran into him at the school when we tried to get information about the two kids who were hurt. We wanted to figure out if it was still safe to send you into that place."

"Mom! You didn't. Of course it's safe."

Dad grunted. "Well, it is and it isn't. In theory, it's safe, but if the majority of students are going to lean in the direction of an idiotic man, more of these 'accidents' are going to happen. I don't want you to end up in the ground like that Harry kid."

"I won't. I'll use my magic defensively. I don't know if he even considered it."

"Good. I may start training you. There are some mental and earth magic tricks that the school doesn't teach."

The offer shocked him. Felix hadn't expected offensive magic lessons as an option. Excitement and apprehension coursed through him. "Okay, Dad, but don't we need to leave? We can discuss all of this after the meeting."

They got into the car and headed to the meeting site. The building was on private land a bit out of town. If you didn't know where it was, you wouldn't stumble upon it. Once there, they found Mr. Elias waiting for them. It was a bit awkward socializing with his teacher, but Felix liked the idea that at least one of his mentors was trustworthy. Though considering what he taught, it wasn't too much of a surprise.

Mr. Elias held out his hand. "Mr. and Mrs. Porter, thank you again for inviting me."

Mom smiled warmly. "Of course. It's always nice to meet another person with a similar outlook on these topics. But please, call us Bonny and Conner."

Mr. Elias smiled. "Excellent, then you'll have to call me Tom."

Felix shivered. There was no way that would be happening. At least, not any time soon. He smiled. "Mr. Elias, if you'll follow us in, we can show you around. Maybe we can introduce you to Vi."

"Vi?"

"She's the leader, at least of this branch of FB Coalition," Felix explained. "She'll be leading the meeting."

They headed in. The main entrance opened into a hallway with a few offices and a set of restrooms. At the end was a set of doors that led into a large conference room. Chairs were set up in rows with an aisle down the center. A small stage with a podium stood at the end. There were maybe forty people in the room, mingling.

"I don't see Vi," Mom said. "We'll take Tom around and introduce him. Why don't you see if there's anything you can do to help out before the meeting."

Felix escaped the adults and circled the area. He found Monte, Vi's assistant, in a corner. She had long, wavy brown hair and wore a brown suit. "Hi, Monte, anything I can do to help?"

Her brown eyes snapped to him, a bit wild. "Felix, oh thank the gods. We have so much to do before this meeting starts. Can you put a flier on each of the seats then come back for more 'to do's? My helpers haven't shown up."

He smiled at her. "Happily."

The two worked until it was time for the meeting to start. He sat with his parents and Mr. Elias half way back. The flier he'd placed told about upcoming events, including the Infinite WISDOM event the following weekend. It gave counter points to the main ones being spread, including fact-checked resources for the counter-points. It was a one-stop-shop of how to talk to the crazies, not that, in Felix's experience, anything ever helped.

Finally, out of a door to the private office in the back, Vi came out. She wore a sky-blue suit, and her brownish-red hair was pinned back. She walked down the center aisle with a purpose. Most days she'd have been out for the meet and greet, so something big must have been going down for her to have missed it.

At the microphone attached to the podium, she stood. "I'm sorry to have missed the start of the meeting. I've had some terrible news. A few of you may know this already." She stared at Felix for a moment as she spoke. "There have been a few assemblies at the school where Tad Shade and his cronies have tried to persuade the students to their side. In many ways, their tactics have worked. But, as you know, there are many students who still think for themselves. A couple of these students, brave students, strong students, thinking students, stood up to question the mouth of Tad Shade at this assembly and for their bravery, they ended up in the hospital, bruised, beaten, and broken."

Vi let her words sink in. Felix had lived this for the last few days and forgot many of the adults wouldn't have known all that had befallen Tansy and Harry.

Once the shock and murmurs stopped, Vi continued. "Of the two students who entered the hospital, only one exited. The goons who work for these people have taken it upon themselves to beat a poor tenth year boy to death. These are the people we are fighting. These are the people we need to keep from power."

A weighty silence filled the air as her words sunk in.

"You have a flier with both links to their talking points and actual sites you can use to counter their arguments. We will stop them. We will find a way to bring reason to ignorance. We will not allow the wanton death of our children."

Applause erupted around the room. Vi continued. "As some of you know, we have someone on the inside who has learned that they're planning to, not only cut the humans out, but create a class system within the magic users. If they are allowed to accomplish what they've started, our world will change in ways we can only begin to imagine."

Chapter 43 - If Looks Could Blow a Person Away

Ember

Monday morning, Ember got to their locker to find a note inside. Grumbling, theya found a request asking them to go to their counselor before first period.

Ember flashed the notice at Daisy and rolled their eyes. "Can you explain to the teacher why I'm late?"

Daisy smiled and nodded. "Of course."

Felix gave them a quick hug before he and Daisy headed off to class.

They watched them go for a moment before they were swallowed up by a horde of students. Spinning on their heel, Ember made their way to the administration wing and found the counselors.

"Oh, Ember, perfect. Mr. Thatcher will see you right away." The too-perky secretary smiled at Ember and pointed to the only open door.

Ember knocked before entering.

A man with short, well-manicured blond hair and blue eyes sat behind a desk. He wore a crisp white button-down shirt and a blue tie that matched his eyes. "Oh, Ember, thank you for coming down here so quickly. I hoped to speak to you before first period. Please have a seat."

"Is there a problem with my classes? Shouldn't I be in earth magic right now?" They sat and stared at the man.

"Oh, no, not really. Well, it seems your performance over the years has left many of us questioning the wisdom in placing you in the discipline in the first place." He gazed at his computer monitor. "But after last Thursday, we think we finally have a solution."

"Last Thursday, sir?" Ember's stomach landed in their gut. "Did I do something wrong?"

"No, no, of course not. I think you finally did something right. That game of catch was amazing. I didn't see it, working down here, but there were many students and so many phones. I got to watch a few recordings. I think the IT club is planning to compile a video from the different uploaded videos to create a movie, you know, for those of us who missed it. Just amazing. Who knew air magic could be so versatile."

Ember sat, uncertain what to say or do. Should they say 'thank you'? Just when they'd decided that was exactly what they should say, Mr. Thatcher continued. "Anyway, your display of air magic has given us the path we needed."

"Oh?" They were shaken out of their ruminations.

"Yes. Mrs. Vintl has requested you come to her class each morning and assist her as her teacher assistant, her TA. Mondays and Wednesdays, she works with ninth years and, as you know, Tuesdays and Thursdays she has a joint tenth and eleventh year class."

It took a few seconds for Ember to catch up with what the counselor meant. "So, you're taking me out of any magic lessons and just having me work as a TA?"

He took a slow breath and nodded. "Well, you'll still be in your potions class. Unless you've been holding back there, we feel you can learn something in that class."

Ember nodded. "Okay, so you've pulled me from my Monday and Wednesday first period earth magic class, and Mrs. Vintl is expecting me up in air magic right now. The rest of my schedule is the same."

He gave them a winning smile. "That about covers it."

"Do my parents know this?"

"Yes, we called them this morning, and they signed off on the schedule change."

They sighed, realizing there wasn't anything else to ask. "Is there anything else, Mr. Thatcher?"

"Only you heading up to class. Have an excellent morning."

As Ember trudged up all the steps to class, the one good thing they decided with this new schedule was they didn't have to deal with Cress and Josie.

They entered the room. Classes had started several minutes before, so Mrs. Vintl was reviewing what the students would be doing for the day.

"You have spent the first part of the year learning how to create twisters. Today you will test with me. I'll be separating you into groups. The test will have three parts. Create a twister, control the speed at which the twister spins, and then control the path it races across the floor. I know not everyone can do all of these skills yet. I need to get you into skill-based groups so everyone can work at the proper pace. As I work with each individual person, I expect the rest of you to practice."

As the students broke up, Mrs. Vintl saw Ember. "Oh, Ember, great." She raised her voice once again. "One last thing, everyone. You all probably know Ember Savita. They are an eleventh year who has agreed to work with me as an assistant. They will help answer questions when there is work time in class, like now. If they offer advice, I suggest taking it, or if you have a question and I am busy, feel free to ask them."

With that, Mrs. Vintl went to the first student on her list and began the testing. Over twenty eyes gaped at Ember as they dropped their bag by the wall and gave a small wave. Raising a brow, they shrugged. "Does anyone have a question?"

Eventually, they all turned away and started practicing. The tension that Mrs. Vintl's words caused began to ebb as Ember circled the class to observe. They really weren't sure what to do. They thought Daisy would be perfect at this.

Most of the class worked in pairs or groups of three, but one girl, petite with ash-blonde hair, sat in the corner by herself. Ember approached. "Hi, my name's Ember. How are you doing?"

The girl's face jerked up, and her bright-gray eyes snapped to Ember's. "I'm fine. I don't have any questions."

"Okay, I just thought, since you aren't working with anyone, maybe we could work together."

Her shoulders slumped. "But you know this already. You don't need to 'work with someone.' You're just mocking me like everyone else."

"Nope, not even a little bit. I find practicing the basics makes the flashy stuff possible."

"Really?" Her eyes narrowed. "Or are you just trying to show off for the teacher?"

"Mrs. Vintl? Naw. I just found out I'm assigned to this class. I don't think I'll be getting out of it too soon. Since I really don't know what I'm doing, I thought if we work together, that would be something."

The girl rolled her eyes. "Fine. Whatever. I get it. You're not leaving until you do something. What do you want me to do?"

"Maybe a twister?"

The animosity pouring off the girl was incredible, but she held out her hand and wiggled her fingers. A small twister appeared on the floor between them.

Face hard and eyes narrow, the girl asked, "Are we good?"

"Can you change the speed of the twister, make it spin faster or slower?"

"No."

Ember squinted. That sometimes helped them to see the air currents. They could almost see the link between the girl and the twister—it was so slight. "If you hold your hand exactly perpendicular, you should be able to use your middle two fingers to control the spinning speed. Your thumb should control the movement speed."

The girl sneered. "Yeah, right. Like you can tell that."

Ember smirked. "Try me."

With a look that defined, 'if looks could kill,' she adjusted her hand then slowly moved first her middle finger then her ring finger. As she did, the speed of the twister first slowed and then sped up. Her hand trembled as her face morphed, jaw slackening and eyes popping open. "How?"

"How what?"

"I've never been able to do that. Mrs. Vintl has tried to help me, but I couldn't figure it out. How did *you*, a mere student who didn't have magic last week, figure it out? I've heard of you. You're a nobody."

Ember bit back the first few comments they wanted to make and settled on, "Well, you're lucky I'm a magicless nobody who happened in on your class."

"Betty Nels," Mrs. Vintl called out.

"Oh, that's me." Her twister dissipated as she ran off to the teacher.

Ember moved to the wall to watch as Betty performed the first part of the test, creating the twister. She then worked through the second, adjusting the speed. Mrs. Vintl whooped with pride. Betty's thumb wiggled, and her face tightened with concentration. The tiny whirlwind crawled a few feet before collapsing.

"That's amazing, Betty. I am so proud of you! You made more progress today than in the last few weeks." Mrs. Vintl moved on to the next student on her list.

Ember decided they were done helping students out. They watched as each student went up to test. Some were pretty good, others no better than Betty. At the end, Mrs. Vintl came over to them. "Thank you for what you did with Betty. I'm not sure what you did, but I worried of ever getting her past just making a twister. You're going to be an amazing helper."

"I'm glad I could assist her."

"I'll see you tomorrow. If you have time after school or if you could come a bit early, maybe we could figure things out. Otherwise, in class will be fine. There will be some work time we can strategize."

Ember nodded and headed to Magical History. They were ready to be a student again.

Chapter 44 - A Strange Request

Ember

In second period, Mr. Elias started class with an announcement. A tenth year had passed away due to a medical condition he'd had since he was born.

Ember raised their hand, but Mr. Elias ignored it. "There's information on the school's website, as well as emails being sent out to your parents. Apparently, Harry

Lows has been sick for some time. His parents informed us his passing doesn't come as a surprise."

They raised their hand more insistently. Felix turned and shook his head. Confused, they put their hand down.

"There will be a memorial service on Wednesday evening for anyone who wants to pay their respects."

Cress snorted. "To a person nobody knew. Why waste our time?"

Ambrose turned on him before anyone else could. "Now's not the time. Someone died."

He shrugged and turned to face the front of the room.

Ember was distracted during class, wondering about the reason Harry's parents gave the school for his death. They'd had a strange first period, and now this. They yearned for a normal day.

After class, Felix waited until everyone filed out. "Harry's parents didn't want his death connected with Infinite WISDOM. They asked everyone involved to use this as the official story."

"But people won't know how unsafe it is to speak up during assemblies. They won't know that the people they support are harming their own."

Felix's jaw tightened for a moment before he exhaled. "I know, but the wishes of the family come first."

Ember's eyes narrowed. "How do you know all of this?"

Mr. Elias, who'd been listening in, came over. "It was discussed at the meeting we attended yesterday."

"You were there?" Ember felt chills at the thought of all the people they knew who went to these meetings.

"Well, to be honest, it was my first time, but it was pretty enlightening."

By lunch, Ember was dismayed at having forgotten to pack a lunch. Standing in line waiting, surrounded by all the other students, the scents, the sounds, Ember just wanted to go and sit and hide.

"There they are, the one that helped me figure out my air magic. It was amazing, like, totally magic! I've been struggling for weeks, and Ember just looked at me and fixed everything. Not even Mrs. Vintl could do that." Betty had a group of friends with her and gazed up at Ember with a wide smile. The look was so different from the one in class, Ember barely recognized the girl.

"Hi, Betty, I'm glad the testing went well for you."

"What'll you have?"

Ember spun away from the gaggle of girls at the sound of the gruff voice. "A slice of pizza and some fries, please."

A tray full of greasy food slapped down in front of them. "What'll you have?"

Ember took the food, moved to the cooler, selected a soda and an apple, and handed their ID card to the cashier. They took a wide path around Betty and crew, and finally made it to their table with Felix. Daisy wasn't there yet. Searching, they saw Daisy paying for her lunch.

"Long day?" The humor in Felix's eyes brought an answering smile from Ember. This was what they needed, distraction and friends.

"You don't know the half of it." They took a bite of pizza and then opened their soda.

Daisy dropped down next to them and sighed. "What happened to you during earth magic class? I wanted to ask sooner, but Simon joined us in potions again, and I just didn't want to talk in front of him. Why *is* he popping up all the time?"

Ember laughed. It felt good. Their friend was cute in her obliviousness. "He must like the company of one of us," Ember hinted.

"Fine, whatever, wait, what? You've got to be kidding me!" Daisy's cheeks burned a bright red.

Felix chuckled. "I don't think they are. Simon isn't joining us for my company or Ember's. Think about it."

"Gods above, I don't think I will. He's so ... arrogant. Let's pretend none of this conversation has happened. Now, Ember, earth magic. That's two classes you've missed in as many weeks. What's up?"

Slumping, Ember explained first about their meeting with Mr. Thatcher, their counselor, and then their first experience as a TA.

Felix snorted. "This lunch is gold. So, you help this Betty student, and they hate you, like really hate you, but you fix whatever issue they've been having."

"Yes?"

"You do know Daisy would be such a better TA than you, right?"

Daisy shimmied and smiled wide.

Ember nodded. "I had that exact thought as I walked around class. Daisy, you would've been in there, helping, bonding, and you would've known everyone in class by the end of it. Me, I just slumped against the wall, waiting for the bell."

From across the table, Daisy placed her hand over Ember's. "I bet it wasn't that bad. I mean, you did help that one girl. And I doubt I'd have thought of that trick you did with the fingers, so there's that."

Felix winked at Ember. "They need both of you, the dream team!"

"That's right," Daisy agreed. "We should petition the school."

A boy came up. Ember wasn't sure if they knew him or not, but he approached the table slowly, watching his feet. He just stood at the edge of the table, not saying anything. Finally Daisy said, "Can we help you?"

He bit his lip, then his tongue darted out. He took a loud breath and said, "I was hoping Ember could unleash my magic like she did with Betty. I can't progress in water magic, and I don't want to be held back."

Both Felix and Daisy had their hands over their mouths, and their bodies shook with their silent laughter. Ember worked to keep their face blank. "I'm not in water magic. I don't know what you think I can do."

"Fix me, like you did for her. She said you're magical."

"I just gave her some ideas to unwind the magic within her. Anyone can do that."

Daisy whispered, "I don't know what you're talking about, Ember, but I don't think that's anything I can do."

The boy looked desperate. "Can you try, please. After school? Please. I'm worried I'll get kicked out."

Felix's warm hand rested on their back. "Why don't we all meet out back after school? We can discuss this unwinding then."

His eyes grew. "Thank you thank you thank you!" He darted away.

Ember's head dropped into their hands. "Gods above, is this a good idea?"

Felix's hand began to rub in a circle, but his voice was full of mirth. "I don't know ... I just don't know."

Chapter 45 - The Dream Team

Daisy

"No me gusta este plan," Ember mumbled as they left Spanish class.

Daisy rolled her eyes. "En Inglés por favor. Gah, now you have me doing it. English!"

Felix chuckled. "Well, we did just leave Spanish class. And why don't you like the plan?"

"I can't fix everyone's magic. I don't know why I figured out Betty's. It was a fluke. I can't go around figuring it out for everyone. I'm guessing that boy will have asked all his friends, and I'm about to make a public spectacle out of myself by doing, wait for it"—Ember waved their hands out to the side—"nothing."

Daisy still couldn't believe their friend, the same one that a week ago was the laughing stock of the school for maybe being 'human,' was now being sought out for magical help. Not only magical help in air magic, apparently any proficiency. *Can Ember help this student? If they can't, people will laugh at them, but that's nothing new, but if they can ... is Ember really the strongest witch in the school? Is that what they've been hiding all these years? If they are, I am in awe of Ember for so many reasons. They are a marvel!*

They got to their lockers, and Ember looked tired. They looked at Felix. "I'm worried. You know what I'm worried about."

When they started dating, Daisy held more of Ember's secrets than Felix. They were tight, best friends, practically siblings. Over the last few months, it had felt like more and more of Ember's secrets had flowed over to Felix. Daisy knew they were dating and that they were serious. Ember's parents liked Felix too, but still, it hurt.

Why doesn't Ember trust me anymore? Did I do something? Does it have to do with those assemblies that

Ambrose and Cress run? Why can't Ember and Felix realize how good that organization would be for the magical community?

The assemblies are about bringing all the magical people together, protecting us from being forgotten. Humans ... no that isn't right, we're human. Humans outnumber us, even if our numbers aren't going down. We can so easily be dismissed. The heart of the group is making sure we're seen, understood, and protected. All those things are good. Why can't my friends see that?

Felix wrapped his hands around Ember's hips. "I know what you're worried about, but I don't think it'll matter. You and your mom together opened this can of worms. In the end, I think this situation will be fine ... *you'll* be fine."

Is Ember worried about what their parents will think about them helping other students? "Did your mom or dad sign off on you being a TA? Because, if they did, your helping out right now should be fine, just an extension of that."

Ember smiled, and it was like the hallway lit up. "You know what, you're right. Thanks, Daisy. You always have the right thing to say."

Daisy smiled back at them and felt things were still good between them.

The three of them headed out to the back of the school. The boy was there with two buckets of water. He'd brought a half dozen friends, including Betty.

Ember studied his setup. "Okay, tell me what you need to do."

He gave a single nod. "Okay, first the water has to arch from one bucket to the other, then I have to create a sphere, and finally I need to separate out a part of the water and make a shape from it, or, preferably, two identical parts."

"It would help if I could see all the steps, just to know if I can even help you." Ember turned to Daisy. "Can you do all of that?"

Daisy winked. "Easy-peasy!" She walked over and held up her hands. She made arc motions, and the water flowed in the same pattern over to the other bucket. Then, she held her hands, palms facing each other, fingers curled as if holding a ball, and pushed her magic out. The water formed a perfect sphere. She wanted to throw a twister in the sphere to show Ember, but not this time. She let the sphere fall and then lifted her right hand to the sky as three small balls of water appeared, each in the shape of a perfect rose. Once they were back in the bucket without a splash, she faced Ember. "Did you get what you needed?"

Ember squinted at the water then at Daisy. "I ... I think so. Thanks. That was really amazing. Okay, you do it."

They pointed at the boy. They really should get a name, but maybe it was too late.

The boy attempted to do the water transfer, but it didn't work. The droplets didn't stay within the shape he tried to hold. Daisy approached him. "You have to hold the shape in here and here." Daisy tapped his forehead and chest. "Head, heart, and soul. You have to feel it, see it, and move it. That's how water works. There is no dorking around. The water knows all."

The boy nodded, and tried again, face scrunched in concentration. This time, it worked.

Daisy smiled. "Good, now, with the sphere, you have to focus hard on the idea that the water will want to escape in every direction, so imagine pulling in ... something. I think of runaway cats, or chocolate chips, depending on how hungry I am. They are running in every direction, and you have to pull them into the center."

He bit his lip. "Okay. Let me try. Pull everywhere to the center." Hands tense, body tense, eyes narrow, his body began to tremble, but he pulled the water to some central point, and a sphere appeared. He started to pant, and then it collapsed. "Oh my gods! Did you see that? I've never done anything like that before. You, you and Ember both, oh gods, that was amazing!"

Daisy preened. She loved helping others and knowing she could be the conduit of their success. "Okay, for the last, imagine your hand is a scoop, just taking what you want. Only when you have it, should you form it."

He tried a few times, but the water wouldn't congeal. It kept splashing back into the bucket. Ember came up to him. "Turn your hand another quarter inch. Flatten your fingers, and push up a bit faster. Once the balls are in the air, use the first two fingers to manipulate and form the spheres or just hold them with this hand and form with your left."

Daisy had no idea what Ember was talking about. Another half inch rotation? Only use two fingers to form something? In all her years, she'd never heard a teacher talk like this. It was beyond bizarro land.

Figuring she'd help the kid in some way if it failed, she watched as he implemented Ember's advice. It shocked her when it worked. Two very sturdy balls floated above the bucket. The kid rotated the pointer fingers of his hands, and the two spheres became cats. Daisy danced in place in excitement. It was perfect.

He let the two water-cats drop into the bucket with a splash and ran over and first hugged Daisy and then Ember. "Thank you both. I don't know what else to say. I'll no longer be the runt in my class. You've unbroken me. Thank you again." He and his friends gathered the water magic supplies and left.

Daisy turned to Ember. "What was all that hand stuff? How did you know?"

Ember shook their head. "I'm not sure. It's just how I feel and see the magic."

Not really sure what Ember meant, Daisy shrugged. "Well, I'm not sure what you mean, but I do know one thing, I was totally right! We are the ultimate dream team!"

Chapter 46 - A Twist of Fate

Ember

When Ember got home, they made a direct line to their room to start homework. They had things to discuss with their parents, but 'teacher expectations' needed to be met. They groaned at their own thought.

They'd worked through three of their classes, texting first Daisy, then Felix to consult on what they were doing, when there was a knock on their door.

They leaned back and rubbed their face. "Yeah?"

Mom came in. "I wanted to talk to you about what happened in school today."

Ember thought about helping that kid with his magic. They never did get his name. Gods above, they'd helped him, worked with him, but didn't even know who he was. *How did Mom learn about that?* "What happened today?"

"Your schedule changing, love. I know it was your first-period class and you had a full day after that, but I figured you'd be thinking about it all day. I'm a bit surprised you didn't text me about it earlier."

They huffed out a laugh. "Oh yeah, that. I'm now a student at Feniks Secondary School for witches and not actually taking any classes on magic. Doesn't that seem, I dunno, wrong somehow?"

The day had been long, but Ember suddenly realized how absurd it all was. At least before when they were teased for being human, they were in earth magic learning ... well, not much. Now it was like they were in school just to socialize. *Maybe I shouldn't complain. Dad will take it as an excuse to pull me out and have us run.*

"You will be in the air magic class as well as Magical Creations and Potions. As for proficiencies, air magic really is the only one you *should* be in. You'll be assisting to teach other students. You'll be amazed at how much more you learn helping others. As you master the minutiae of the basics, I can really push the other end and challenge you on advanced techniques on the weekends."

"Can we work with Daisy as well? She asked if you'd tutor her too."

Mom's eyes danced as she smiled. "I think that sounds lovely." Her face slowly shifted to something more neutral. "Now, you seemed confused when I came in here. What else happened today?"

Ember explained about how they saw the magic between both Betty and the boy and their workings. "Is that ... normal? Can you do that? I could see it, and tell how their movements were hampering the effect they wanted to achieve."

"Hmm." Mom's brow wrinkled in thought. "I've never heard of anything like that. You with your phoenix sight and witch abilities ... you are something wholly new. I don't know that anyone can do what you do."

"Should I hide my help? I mean, I don't know if it's too late. I helped two students."

"In Mrs. Vintl's class? I mean, helping air magic students seems fine. It's what you're in there to do. I don't really see any issues with that."

Ember sank deeper into their seat. "One of the kids was a water mage."

Mom grumbled, "How did that happen, Ember?"

They explained. Then, they explained again in the kitchen to both Mom and Dad. Dad shook his head. "Every time something can go wrong. We should've run. It's too late now. In less than a week, you've gone from a magicless anomaly to this powerhouse who can magically fix everyone. Great. Well, we will see how it plays out. At least it's all in the world of magic. I'm fine with that. Just try to avoid fire."

You're fine with it, but I'm the one who has to deal with ... everyone. "Great! Sounds like a plan."

Dad laughed. "You don't sound like you really think it'll be great. But I think you can handle it, dear."

The next day, Ember walked up to air magic with Daisy. They joked as they entered the room a half hour before class started.

Mrs. Vintl smiled when she saw Ember, looked confused at seeing Daisy, then shrugged and smiled. "Daisy, why don't you sit and wait while Ember and I discuss today's class."

Daisy smiled wide. "Of course, Mrs. Vintl. Sounds perfect!"

Ember put their bag next to Daisy and met their teacher on the other side of the large room. "Are we just continuing the lesson from last Tuesday?"

"Yes, but, well, I was hoping you could go around over the next few classes and work with each of the students and help them the way you helped Betty yesterday. I'm not sure what you said or did with her, but, well, it was amazing. She's been struggling to get a basic twister since the start of the school year, and yesterday you got her, not only able to create one, she controlled it in both the basic maneuvers. She isn't our strongest ninth year, but that only takes confidence."

Ember had to fight years of self-conditioning and hiding. This was why the school and Mrs. Vintl asked them to be an assistant, and last night both their parents gave them a thumbs up for doing just this. *Everything is fine as long as I excel in magic. Show the world our family is amazing witches. If they see us as witches, how could we be anything else?*

Taking a calming breath, Ember nodded and then smiled. "Yeah, I can do my best."

"That's all anyone can ever ask you to do. It's nice seeing this side of you, Ember. Never hide who you are."

If she only knew.

Ember and Daisy were sitting and talking as the rest of the class filed in. Once the bell rang, Mrs. Vintl started class. "Now that we all know that what I asked you to do with the platforms is possible, we will continue to focus on floating the notebooks."

"Why is Ember even still *in* our class? They obviously don't need to learn any of this." Simon's mocking voice rang out from the other side of the few students in attendance.

"That is an excellent question. Ember will be helping me help you. You are correct, they've been holding back, trying to learn the basics. Well, they've learned them, and now they can help you to master some of the trickier aspects of air magic."

Simon scoffed. "I doubt they can teach me anything. A one-trick pony doesn't a good teacher make."

Ember shrugged. "For someone bent on being the best, who knew your arrogance would get in the way of learning? I'll avoid helping you, no worries."

He glared but didn't say anything else. When class began, Ember started off watching to get a feel of how everyone was doing. They eventually worked with one of the tenth years who they knew struggled the most, Rane Cole. He usually came in last in the warm-up.

As everyone created a twister on their colored circles, Rane's small twister just missed his yellow target. His face twisted better than the air he created, and he waved his hands until it got to where he wanted it. Then he moved, somewhat spasmodically, until the small thing crossed the floor to the end point. It only missed hitting the other twisters because all the others were across the room and dissipated.

"Okay, everyone. Get your bricks and a notepad, and start the next stage of class."

With only seven students working, everything was quiet. In the Monday class, everyone was in the same grade, and it was noisy. Working with Betty had been relatively private. Ember walked over to Mrs. Vintl. "Could I work with a student in the hall, you know, to not embarrass them, or me?"

She shook her head. "That isn't the best idea, but that door leads to a private practice room. We haven't needed it with your class, too small. You could work with students individually in there."

They went over to Rane and squatted next to him. "I was wondering if we could work together in the private practice space."

His eyes narrowed, and it looked like he was about to say no, but then he shrugged. "It isn't like I'm getting anywhere with this, anyway. Should I bring the setup?"

"Sure. Why not." Ember shrugged.

Everyone watched as they headed to the private room. Simon guffawed. "Too scared of failure to work out here, Ember? You're such a hack!"

"Are you so threatened by people better than you, Simon, or is it people you perceive as female?" Daisy chuckled.

He blanched. "Ember isn't better than me. Not last week, not today, never."

Ignoring them, Ember led Rane towards privacy. It was about the quarter of the size of a regular classroom, bigger than they'd expected. "Why don't you put that stuff in the corner for now. I want to start with your twister."

"My what? Why?"

"Just ... I have an idea."

He sighed and contorted his body until the tiny thing appeared.

"Right, let it go. Stand up tall, put out both your hands, no, both hands at angles, like you're making a roof of a house. Yes, like that. Now, with your middle fingers, make the letter O, and push out your magic."

He did, and the twister reappeared, a bit bigger and steady. His eyes widened. "Oh my gods. How did you do that?"

"I didn't. You did. Now, try wiggling each finger individually and together. Figure out what you can do."

Ember watched as Rane figured out his magic and his control. Over the next half hour, his confidence grew, and with it, so did his control.

"I think if you set up your bricks and notepad, the density of air will correlate with making a fist. The lifting will be with rotating that fist, palm up to the ceiling, opening your hand, and lifting. I'm not positive, but that's where I'd start. I think you're good to rejoin class."

They walked out, and Simon snorted. "Class is almost over. Can you do anything you couldn't before going in there, Rane? Or did you just waste all that time?"

He put down his stuff and held out his hands. He created a twister that ran across the room faster than anyone had ever seen it move. Everyone stared at where the small bit of air disappeared then at him, smiling ear to ear. "It was mostly a waste. You're ever so clever, Simon, as always."

Chapter 47 - Throwing down the Gauntlet

Ember

Wednesday evening, Harry's family held a memorial service for him.

Ember attended with Felix and Daisy. Inside the building was a vestibule with a table and a book for signing in. They each signed their name. They found seats halfway up. Ember noticed several familiar faces but not as many as they'd expected.

An older man walked up to the podium. He stood tall, but his face was drawn and tired-looking. "I'd like to thank you for coming to remember my son. As you know, he was our only son. He was smart, had a few good friends, and never followed what others said without deciding for himself if the path presented seemed right for him. Every day, his mother and I were proud of the man he was growing up to be. In grade eight, he went out and got an apprenticeship as a lab assistant at a hybrid science company. They told him, 'We don't usually work with kids so young.' He replied, 'Try me out. It's free labor. What do you have to lose?' Three years later, they told me he was one of the brightest stars they had. They couldn't imagine ... can't imagine running that place without him." His eyes watered, and he took out a handkerchief to blow his nose.

A woman, a bit thicker than the man and wearing a beautiful black dress, came up to him. She looked as if she held herself tight, unwilling to show her grief. "It'll be okay. He died fighting for a cause he believed in." Blushing, she turned to the people watching them. "Harry believed in our world, the peace between magic users and humans. He knew ... *he knew* that the only way forward was for that peace to continue. He spent years working with every type of person out there. The idea of this animosity existing was anathema to what we all know. His death is just the beginning. I hope those of you with kids won't be standing where we are in the near future, and those of you who are kids ... be careful, but don't lose your way."

Daisy whispered close to Ember's ear. "I thought he died of a medical condition. The school's report proved what Tansy thought was wrong, right?"

Ember shook their head. "Later."

The dad sighed. "We appreciate all of you being here. There are refreshments in the next room and a microphone if anyone else would like to share any words about Harry."

Daisy said she had to leave. Her mom needed her help for a home project. Ember saw her eyes were red-rimmed with her grief and knew that they must look similar. Ember hugged their friend and said they'd call her later.

Everyone else moved to the room with round tables and buffet-style food. Ember and Felix filled their plates and sat at an edge table. Soon, they were joined by Tansy, Olivia, and a few other people Ember didn't know. They started eating and everyone got quiet.

A sound from outside caught Ember's attention. Dread shivered down their spine. They grabbed Felix's hand and headed to a window. Outside, across the street, were a group of people with picket signs. On the signs read, 'Down with human lovers,' 'Witches First,' 'Infinite WISDOM,' and more and more.

Bile rose in the back of Ember's throat. Thoughts of wind and fire flashed in their mind.

Before they could take any action, Harry's dad took up the microphone. "We are here to remember and say goodbye to Harry. We ask that everyone ignore the protesters. We don't want a fight today." His eyes narrowed as he gazed to where the Shade followers stood outside the venue. "Tomorrow, however, is another story."

Chapter 48 - Next Time, Knock

Ember

The school part of the week went by smoothly. Ember was thrilled it was finally Friday. Helping students in air magic got easier. Each class, they focused on one student. Mrs. Vintl seemed to approve of this approach. Both Betty and Rane were working on the advice given earlier in the week, so Ember chose new victims ... er, students to help.

On Friday during study hall, they could enjoy first period with their friends. Tansy and Olivia joined them, and they did as much talking as studying. No one in class seemed to care.

As students came into class, Ember saw a few wearing shirts with infinity signs on them. Some just had a small sign near the shoulder; some had big ones across the chest. On those, each oval of the sideways-looking eight had an image. In the left oval was a bubbling cauldron; in the right, a not equal sign. Tracing the curve of the left side of the infinity sign was the word 'infinite.' Under the not equal sign was the word 'WISDOM.'

"Are you going to the city-wide assembly tomorrow?" Tansy asked after seeing the third student walk in wearing one of these shirts.

Ember worked to keep their face blank. "Yeah, I think so."

Tansy shook her head. "I thought about it and decided I'd catch the highlight on the ten-o'clock news or from friends later on. I've had enough of that ... malarky to last me some time."

Olivia nodded. "I could come over and hang out with you. We could take a walk. We'd have the town to ourselves."

"Sure, but I'd like to stay in. I just don't trust being 'out' during one of those assemblies."

Daisy huffed. "I think you're overreacting. I mean, stay home, don't go, all of that is fine. But don't stay in because of fear. These people are about lifting magic users up."

Tansy narrowed her gaze at Daisy. "Did you see the picketers at Harry's memorial service?"

"What picketers?"

Olivia frowned. "No, Daisy left before the protesting started. She missed all the excitement."

"Will someone tell me what you're talking about?"

Tansy filled her in.

Daisy rolled her eyes. "You have to be exaggerating. The Infinite WISDOM group wouldn't support any of that. Were Ambrose or Cress there? They're the face of this movement. If they weren't there, it was probably humans trying to give the group a bad name. Did you even think about that?"

Everyone paused, mouths open slightly, gaping at her. What could they say?

Ember was still debating ways to get Daisy to see reason when they headed to gym a few periods later. They'd gotten into the pattern of taking a small bag of gym clothes and slipping into the bathroom. There was a single-room stall with a locking door they'd been using as a changing room, and so far, no one else seemed to notice. The locker room was mostly about getting in and out and on your way.

Ember had just slid out of their jeans and was folding them to fit into the small clothes bag when the door flew open. Their heart stopped as they realized they'd forgotten to lock it in their haste to get dressed. With a snap of their head, they looked into the eyes of Ambrose, jaw to the floor gaping at them. Her eyes raked over their exposed body.

Ember spun, grabbed their shorts, and slipped them on. "Excuse me. I'll be done in a minute." They shut the door, made sure to lock it, and changed their top.

Heart pounding in their chest, they opened the door and marched past Ambrose to their locker. Once their stuff was secure, they headed out to the field.

Throughout gym class, they waited for a comment from Ambrose, but one never came.

Chapter 49 - The Worst Kind of Accident

Ember

The weather Saturday morning was bright, sunny, and warm. Ember decided to wear a skirt and a T-shirt. It would be cooler than jeans. They wondered how many people would come to the city-wide event, hundreds? Thousands? A shiver went down their spine.

In the kitchen, Dad had prepared eggs, bacon, hash browns, and pancakes. Their stomach spoke its approval of the meal. They headed for the coffee maker, selected the largest mug they could find, then filled two plates, one with everything but the pancakes, and a second with the sweet stuff.

Dad's plate was almost empty. "Are you ready for today? It could get ugly, but it's about time your mom and I see the message ourselves."

"Well, the message will be ugly, that's for sure. I've already experienced it twice."

He grunted in agreement.

Mom, sitting between Ember and Dad, took a bite of pancake. "At least you know their message probably won't change very much. It will be interesting to see who goes and the expressions they make. You know who supports and who opposes, though, it may not always be obvious."

Ember held their coffee in both their hands, savoring the smell and taste of their favorite morning brew. "I just wish we knew how to stop this. I worry it's a snowball effect and nothing short of a miracle will kill the movement. If putting kids in the hospital didn't affect its popularity, nothing will."

Mom nodded. "But you told us that Tansy and Harry's injuries were spun to be something else, not the fault of Infinite WISDOM. Their supporters don't know that their own organization is harming witches, at least, not yet."

Ember made a disapproving face at that comment but couldn't dispute it. They finished eating and got ready to go.

The event was being held downtown, just over a mile from their house, and they figured parking would be nearly impossible. They chose to walk. As they got closer, they realized they'd made the right choice as cars zoomed around trying to find places to land.

They agreed to meet Felix's family near the café, and both groups found a spot not too close to the set up stage. The air around the event was electric, with speakers set up and people milling about. Vendors had stands, where they had shirts, hats, pins, and other paraphernalia to sell. Ember watched as people bought the souvenirs, as well as balloons and light sticks.

Finally, the event started. They had a long list of speakers, and part of Ember wished they hadn't come. *I want to know what lies are being spread, but a full day of this?*

"The witches need to band together and raise their children up, ensuring their future to be the brightest future it can be!"

"The humans have had two hundred years to see our power. Their jealousy has led to their desire to bring us down."

"History was written by the winners. Were any of you there at the War of Peace to know how the victors and losers really panned out? Were any of you truly in the meeting of ten that came up with those laws? We must create laws that work with the people of today and fit the witches of today!"

"The humans are hoping we don't notice that their population has grown exponentially while ours has not. They want to smother us by sheer numbers. They think we won't notice when they bury us and take away our political might. But we do notice, and their machinations will not work!"

It went on and on. Many statements sounded good, but when looked at closely, it all lead to hate and genocide. When the crowd yelled in unison, Ember would sometimes say what they really thought. "Humans and witches are equal, and you're ignorant."

They stood between Felix and their mom, and no one else could hear them. After their second statement, said in a mocking speaking voice, not a yell, Felix leaned over. "As much as I agree, it's probably best to not say those things here and now. I know I'm being paranoid, but Harry is still on my mind."

Ember saw Dad's nod in their peripheral vision.

They sighed. "Okay, fair."

When the debacle ended, crowds cheering, feet stomping, Ember turned to their parents. "Can Felix and

I walk back in through the park? There are just too many people here."

Dad searched the crowd. "Sure, You'll get most of the way home before you two separate. By then, you'll be far enough from the crazies. I'm good with that. Just remember, both of you, you can defend yourselves ... magically."

They nodded and headed out.

Once away from the people, they cut towards the walking path. Felix hooked his arm in theirs. "That was ... a lot."

"I can't believe they had eight speakers and the crowd stayed engaged the whole time. It isn't like what they said changed. Why are so many magic users ready for separation from humans?"

"I don't know." Felix shook his head. "It isn't like a friendship between them and us harms us. It isn't like a representational government has harmed the magic users. Yes, there are fewer of us in political power, but there would be ways to change that, and no laws have come out that harm witches."

"They will if this movement doesn't end. It will force humans to realize the situation they're in." They walked for a few minutes, then Ember shook their head. "You know, I hate that designation, though it's been used forever. I'm human, you're human, we're magic users, and non-magic users. Why can't we do something with that?"

Felix laughed. "I love that you can always make me laugh. Probably too long of a title."

They got to the point of the path where their houses lay in different directions. Felix pulled them in, placing his hands on their hips. "Did I mention how nice you look in your skirt?"

They smiled. "No, you didn't."

"Well, you do. Maybe later tonight, I could take you out on a proper date. It's been awhile."

"Maybe. Let me go see what all's happening at home today."

He nodded then pulled them in for a kiss. "Talk soon. Stay safe."

"You too."

They watched Felix turn off on the side path before continuing towards home. The path was wide, and they listened to the birds sing. The breeze felt nice after the stuffy feeling of being near all the people for the last hour or so. They stretched their legs and walked a bit faster.

A man stepped out from the trees ahead of them. Taller than Ember by a few inches, broad, and thick with muscles. They tried to step around him—the path was wide enough—but two other men caught their arms.

Ember jerked. "Let me go!"

"I don't think so." His voice slithered out. "We saw your discontent at the assembly. We know you're a human lover, thinking they're as good as us. You don't believe in the new world Mr. Shade is building for us."

The two men punched them in the sides. Through the pain, Ember kicked out, aiming for their knees. A life of training took over, and they got one with a solid hit, and he fell hard.

The man facing them ran in with a knife he'd pulled out since Ember last looked at him. They saw the moment the 'accident' happened. *Why is the magic of a phoenix to always force the worst to happen?* He tripped on a rock, and fell towards Ember, the knife embedding in their chest.

Pain erupted everywhere, and they fell to the ground, suddenly released. Blurry vision showed the men backing away.

"What do we do? We weren't supposed to kill her."

Their vision slowly was blacking out.

"Something, we killed that boy, another mistake and we're toast."

Trembling broke out throughout Ember's body.

"Fire, you have fire. Burn the evidence. She'll just go missing."

Ember wanted to laugh as they felt their clothing catch fire.

Chapter 50 - The War of Peace

Ember

Ember woke up, cold, naked, and thankfully alone. They were surrounded by blackened ground off the path surrounded by trees. They pushed up to sitting and searched for anything they could use to cover up. Nothing. They were at least a half mile from home, and most of that was residential. They could turn invisible but only in bird form.

Well, there's no hope for it. I'll have to shift. Maybe I can get Mom or Dad outside, and they can let me into the garage to shift back. This isn't good. Idiot Infinite WISDOM goons.

Ember closed their eyes and felt for the fire and feathers within themself. With a push, they let their feathers free. There wasn't pain, just a release as the bird burned through their soul and they shot towards the sky, settling invisibility over themself as they ascended.

They circled downtown. As long as they were in the sky, may as well see what was still happening at the assembly spot. Ember gazed down at the people milling around the stage. Their eyesight was perfect in this form, and they could see the smallest of details. Ambrose stood with her father and Mr. Shade. Ember wished they could hear what they talked about.

Near one of the vendors that sold shirts and knickknacks, Ember saw Daisy and Simon. Their gut clenched at the sight. *Why is Daisy falling for this hogwash? It's utter crud! She's so much smarter than this, better than this. Even Simon should know better.* It looked like they were pawing through the shirts. Ember wanted to hurl.

They turned and flew in the direction of Felix's house, realizing if they'd been attacked, it was possible Felix had been as well. They retraced the path he would've taken all the way to his house but didn't see him. Ember circled his house, but ... nothing. They darted home and rang the doorbell. When Dad answered, they rang the bell again. "Ember?"

They dared a small flare of fire, then tamped it out.

He grumbled, "In the garage. It's the only safe place." The door closed, and the garage door opened. Ember waited while Mom pulled the car out. Then, they waddled in.

After a few moments, the door shut, and they dropped the invisibility.

Mom sighed as Dad came out with a shirt and a skirt. Ember shifted. The change hurt a bit more, the bird always wanting to be free, never wanting to give up its wings. The burning stung as they forced the fire to hide the wings behind the skin of a person.

Once they were back in their skin, Mom made a pained sound. "Tell us what happened."

Ember slid on their clothes. "Let me call Felix first. I need to make sure he's okay."

Once Ember knew he was home and safe, they told their parents the full story.

"So, they were the same goons that got Harry?" Dad grumbled, leading them into the kitchen.

"Yeah, that's what it sounds like."

Dad moved to the refrigerator and started making Ember a sandwich. "You know, I don't know that we can keep pretending we're not involved. You heard the stuff those speakers were spewing. It felt personal."

"What do you want to do, Ash? We've stayed under the radar for years, decades even."

Dad placed the plate with a sandwich, chips, and a soda in front of Ember. "We're going to join the fight. That meeting, the one run by FB Coalition, we're going to go tomorrow. I can't believe FB has stayed alive all these years and morphed into something legitimate. I wonder who had the gall to do that?"

Ember put down their half eaten ham and cheese. "What does FB stand for? Why do you know it?"

Leaning back in his seat, Dad got a far off look to his face, a smile slowly creeping over the corners of his mouth. "It started when I was young. Well, not that young. We knew the war was getting worse and the phoenixes had to have a hand in running it. We were old, your grandparents, uncles, cousins, very old. Other shapeshifters came to us and asked us to help. There were some witches who had amassed some abilities that they couldn't stop, and they knew our fire was the only thing that could end the fighting that would otherwise kill all but the very strongest of the magic users."

Ember shook their head. "Wait, I've never learned that. There were witches that wanted to kill other magic back then?"

Mom nodded. "Yes. The power being thrown around was taking out full towns. The young, the old, everyone was dying in droves. It's the real reason the humans learned about us. It couldn't be hidden at that level of use. A few magic users tried to stop the tide, but it was useless. The truly powerful were set on a course of self-destruction. They thought they were purifying the race to start anew."

Dad shivered. "It was disgusting what they wanted. If they had their way, no one, witch, human, or shapeshifter, would've survived. We started a group, my sister Nuri and I, the Fire Bird Coalition, FB. The phoenixes joined, then the shapeshifters. In the end, witches joined us as well, the good ones. That was when I met your mother. Her branch of magic, the spatial magic users, all joined. They were part of the vanguard. A few did survive. You and your mom may not be the only two out there, but trumpeting the ability wouldn't be safe, even in the peace of the last two hundred years. Not until there are enough practitioners that it's considered somewhat normal."

Ember's head spun. "Why isn't any of this taught?"

Mom shrugged. "We discussed it in the aftermath of the war. We decided letting the general population know that there were witches with that sort of power could and would only lead to copycat antics. So in the end, we decided to start the story at the finish, with the cleanup."

"History is written by the victors, indeed." Ember snorted.

Chapter 51 - A Meeting of Friends

Ember

When Ember opened the door, they found Felix standing with a smile and a bouquet of flowers. They'd called him again after their talk with their parents. First, they wanted to fill him in on their walk home, then to tell him they'd be attending the meeting.

"I'm so glad to see you're okay, though I guess that's a given with you. And another skirt. Maybe we can have that date we missed last night tonight?"

Warmth blossomed within Ember. "Yeah, maybe."

"So, I'm here to escort your family to the meeting today. I know you and your family could've driven by yourself, but I thought I could just tag along."

"I'd like that." Ember smiled, putting the flowers he brought in a glass with water.

Mom came up next to them. "Sounds like a plan. We should be ready in a minute, and since Ember needed the garage yesterday, the car is in the driveway."

Felix reached out and wrapped his fingers around theirs. They headed to the car and slid into the back seat to wait for Ember's parents. It didn't take long, and they were off.

Dad backed out of the driveway. "Who did you say ran these meetings?"

Felix watched Dad through the rearview mirror. "A woman named Vi. She's great. You'll love her. She's been our leader as long as my family has been going. She has an assistant named Monte, who I usually help." He turned to Ember. "Maybe we can help her today. I usually do any odd job that needs getting done while the adults mingle. I mean, chit chatting with adults is great and all ..."

Ember laughed. "I think I'll stick with you. Helping out sounds a tad bit better."

Mom rotated in her seat to stare at Felix. "How many people usually come to these meetings?"

Felix narrowed his eyes and gazed up towards the ceiling of the car. "I'd say a month ago it was maybe thirty. In the last few weeks, the numbers have been growing. We have maybe doubled our numbers as the assemblies at school and now downtown have happened. As popular as Tad Shade's message is to many, there are a lot of people who are bristling under the idiocy."

Dad grunted his agreement as he pulled into the parking lot. There were a lot of cars, but he found a spot. The Center was outside of town in a remote area. Ember turned and tried to see if there was anything they recognized around them. "This place is a bit ... lonely, don't you think? Maybe I've seen too many horror movies, but, isn't this where they all take place?"

Felix laughed. "You have your movies mixed up. This is the secret hide out of the good guys. Now, inside with you." His warm hand clasped theirs, and they headed for the door. They met up with his parents along the way, and they pawned off Ember's parents with his, leaving them to find Monte to help.

The first hallway they entered was long and well lit. Several shut doors, Felix explained, led to offices. At the end, they entered a meeting hall, and Ember was almost overwhelmed with the number of people. They leaned into Felix. "There are not enough seats for the number of people in here. This is ludicrous."

His eyes looked ready to pop from his head. "You're telling me. I've never seen this many people at one of these events. Come on, we need to find Monte. She's probably freaking out right about now." He dragged them through the crowd until they found a woman with long, wavy brown hair in a well-put-together blue suit. Her brown eyes looked a bit wild.

"Felix, thank the gods. Okay, we need all the chairs, like, all of them. They're in the back. There are a few others getting them set up, but gods above, how are there so many people here? When you're done, come back."

They were about to turn when she stopped them. "Wait, who's that. I don't have any workers I don't know."

"This is my friend and who I'm dating. Their name is Ember."

Monte held out a hand. "It's a pleasure to meet you, and later we can do something more formal, I'm sure. I'm Monte, and thank you for helping!"

They ran off to gather chairs. Once done, they placed fliers on the seats, then water bottles beneath. Then, they got to sit in the seats.

Ember sat between Felix and their dad. Their mom sat in the row ahead with Felix's parents. They would've taken the full row, but people filled in too fast.

Monte walked to the microphone in a podium on the stage facing all the seats. "Hi, everyone. To those of you who are new, my name is Monte Winter. I've been working with Vi for ... well, for a long time. This group, FB Coalition, has been around, in one way or another, for years, centuries even. If you want the full history, we can go into it after the meeting. I don't know that all of you want it, but we do know our group's origins."

Ember thought about that as they noted Dad's brow raise. He mumbled, "I wonder if they really do. We may just have to stay to find out."

Monte waited out the small talk then continued. "We here at FB Coalition work towards keeping the peace, to put it simply. We know what happens when magic and magic users get too powerful. So, to get to the topic for today, I would like to bring out Vi, my partner, our founder, and our leader."

Applause broke out, and Ember turned to see the door on the back wall open. A woman wearing a green business-appropriate dress came out. She had hair almost the same color as theirs, pinned up on the sides. She took two steps towards them before Ember felt Dad move.

His voice rumbled through the quiet of the room. "Nuri? You're here?"

The woman's eyes widened, and her mouth started to open before she snapped it shut. The sides twitched as her head tilted. Ember could only imagine the thoughts tumbling through her mind.

Next to Ember, Felix whispered, "What am I missing?"

Ember said, "She's my aunt."

Thank you for reading Veiled Phoenix!
Please leave a review online.

Check out my website to find all the links to my socials
and find information on my next series!

Coming up:
- Moonstone Phoenix

- Battle Phoenix

- Pebble's Story

  o Xenagogue

  o Yugen

  o Zephyr

About the Author

Huckleberry Rahr is a mathematics instructor at the University of Wisconsin-Whitewater. She spent many years teaching math around the Midwest and in Papua New Guinea with the Peace Corps. Her parents  instilled a love of reading from a young age.

She grew up with lesbian moms who had a huge collection of women authors with heroines as the protagonist. Her favorite genre was fantasy and science fiction, that is, until she discovered urban fantasy. What her mom's library lacked were books with characters that looked like her family: diversity in background, gender identity, and sexuality. She decided if she couldn't find that series, then she would write it.

www.ingramcontent.com/pod-product-compliance
Lightning Source LLC
Chambersburg PA
CBHW020237010826
48973CB00006B/1544

9781959981589